To my —

"Jack Armstrong is an engaging storyteller, whose narratives are shaped by a lifetime of practicing internal medicine and exploring faith. He invites the reader to enter into the complex interaction of scientific data and protocol, family dynamics, diverse personal needs and motivations, legal considerations, and ethical dilemmas in the practice of modern medicine. These stories make the case for the critical role of doctors and medical professionals who are attentive to patients and shaped by humanitarian impulses to negotiate these interactions. They are a graphic reminder that medicine really is an art as well as a science."

—RICHARD W. REIFSNYDER

Author of *Surprised by Christmas: Stories Told Through Advent and Christmas*, and *The Pilgrimage of Faith*

"Dr. Armstrong's raw, emotional recounting of his career in the medical field gives a peek behind the curtain for readers as a doctor wrestles with questions, the everyday demands of working the medical field, and faith."

—AMANDA MAGUIRE THOMAS

Associate Pastor, First Presbyterian Church, Winchester

"Jack Armstrong and I practiced medicine together for over thirty years and have been friends for longer. His collection of short stories is a poignant glimpse into a seldom-seen side of medicine and reflects what we as health care providers consider the essence of practicing medicine. . . . These stories go beyond traditional diagnosis and treatment, portraying what is really important in our lives. Well worth the read."

—PHILIP O'DONNEL

President, Selma Medical Associates

"The sign of a gifted raconteur is the ability to paint the broad brushstrokes of a piece of art, allowing the reader to fill in the rest of the canvas with imagination. The author does just that in these stories. With his use of rich metaphor and creative turns of phrase, he delights with his talent for storytelling. With each poignant story taken from his life in medicine, he invites the reader to witness the beauty and pathos of the human condition. I highly recommend that you take the time to enjoy and be inspired by these stories from Dr. Jack Armstrong."

—DEBORAH KAISER-CROSS

Author of *Sacred Moments,* and *Prayers Through the Seasons.*

"If you are a healthcare worker, please read this book! Jack's stories are a strong reminder of the symphony of experiences, attitudes, values, commitments, and cultural patterns which accompany every person seeking healing or support at your healthcare institution—a symphony that needs to be listened to, understood, and honored as you interact with the person who is entrusted to your care."

—PETER FORD

Chaplain, Winchester Medical Center

LION IN THE NIGHT

LION IN THE NIGHT

STORIES

JACK ARMSTRONG

Foreword by John R. Perfect
Illustrations by Lena Rodriquez Gillett

RESOURCE *Publications* · Eugene, Oregon

Resource Publications
An Imprint of Wipf and Stock Publishers
199 W. 8th Ave., Suite 3
Eugene, OR 97401

www.wipfandstock.com

PAPERBACK ISBN: 978-1-5326-7436-5
HARDCOVER ISBN: 978-1-5326-7437-2
EBOOK ISBN: 978-1-5326-7438-9

Manufactured in the U.S.A.   04/18/19

To my patients, who instructed me in the school of life.
To Christine, my wife, who encouraged and edited my early
writing efforts. To my children, Andy, Matt and Katee who
read, laughed and gently guided my storytelling.
To editor Daniel, who gave structure and guidance
to the publishing experience.

CONTENTS

FOREWORD BY JOHN R. PERFECT | ix

INTRODUCTION | 1

KNIFE | 2

I THOUGHT YOU WERE ALONE | 8

A DETROIT MAN | 12

HERO | 16

LUNAR NIGHTS | 21

SPECIAL GIRLS DAY | 31

JACKSON HOLE | 54

FA'A SAMOA | 60

THE FINAL SHOCK | 73

CLARE | 78

VOICES | 88

THE LAST CHILD | 93

LION IN THE NIGHT | 101

LAST WORDS | 108

ROXIE | 114

FEVER | 117

HUNTED | 122

AN ANGEL | 129

BIOGRAPHY | 135

Foreword

L ion in the Night is a compilation of short stories from the medical practice of Dr. Jack Armstrong. In this set of stories Dr. Armstrong provides a personal account of his interactions with patients and life's issues during healing. They provide clear, entertaining and humble visions and principles about healing through the lens of a physician caregiver.

Dr. William Osler summarizes the following about the medical profession. "I would rather tell you of a profession honored above all others; one which while calling forth the highest powers of the mind, brings you into such warm personal contact with your fellow men that the heart and sympathies of the coldest nature must needs be thereby. Will not your whole energies be spent in befriending the sick and suffering? in helping those who cannot help themselves? in rescuing valuable lives from the clutch of grim death? in cheering the loving nurses of the sick, who often hang upon your words with a most touching trust? Aye![1]

Osler describes Dr. Armstrong and his profession. The medical profession is truly a gift for those who enter into the ethical/ moral contact of dealing with human misery. Dr. Armstrong simply and elegantly describes through his cases in this book that despite all the technology and knowledge, the clinician's gift is caring for his or her patients in need (one at a time and necessarily entering into their private space). The medical profession must

---

1. Counsels and Ideals from the writings of William Osler and selected aphorisms. *The Classic of Medicine Library*. Birmingham. pp 129 -30, 1985.

never forget this gift of care and the special relationship it holds with patients' health. Despite all the CT/ MRI scans and electronic medical records today, nothing will substitute for listening to the patient! This is Dr. Armstrong's message and career; it is well described in this book which is useful to caregivers and patients alike. Human misery will continue but healing starts with the gifts of medical professional like Dr. Armstrong who listen and care.

John R. Perfect, MD
James B. Duke Professor of Medicine
Chief, Division of Infectious Diseases
Duke University Medical Center

INTRODUCTION

A physician's life might be viewed as hard and demanding or blessed, depending on one's perspective. Certainly the intense training period is hard and demanding, lasting over a decade past college for some physicians. Adding to the work demands is the natural and trained desire to never make a mistake in diagnosis or treatment that adds to a patient's suffering.

So how is a physician's life blessed? Blessed is he by the permission granted by patients to enter into their lives at the most private, personal, and deepest levels. This permission is granted in part from the patient's need to understand and treat their illness, but also in part from trust earned from years of confident interaction. With this trust the physician may be witness to extraordinary courage, dramatic events, and remarkable challenges, often in faraway places.

The extraordinary people who speak to you in these stories have a truth to tell. Some of these truths are spoken, but others are acted out in the caldron of everyday life. As witness to these truths, I hope to convey the patients' stories—and mine—to add a new lens to the reader's eye into the meaning of life.

Remember, my readers, these stories are 100 percent fiction and 99 percent true.

KNIFE

Lynn shifted in her chair, her black, short-haired head bobbing up and down in anger.

"You did this, didn't you?" she hissed.

I remained silent as only a guilty, ten-year-old boy is capable of doing.

"How am I supposed to take notes without a pencil?" she asked. "If I tell Mr. Hubbard I can't take notes because someone broke off all my pencil ends, he'll know it was you. And you know how hot he gets!" Mr. Hubbard was a large former Marine who was capable of great feats of anger and placing offending students under his desk when provoked.

I reached over Lynn's shoulder and placed a sharp pencil in her now-outstretched hand.

As we exited the fifth grade classroom, Gordon was visible, leaning against the cinderblock wall of Vetal Elementary School. Gordon was a full foot taller than me, and a notorious, crude prankster. His smirk told me I was his next victim.

"Going to play a little baseball today, Armstrong?" he asked.

"Yeah, after I get my mitt, Gordon," I said as I tried to slip by him.

Gordon reached out a long arm to block me. "Good luck finding your mitt, Armweak," Gordon said.

I turned to face Gordon, a quick memory of my brother's fighting lesson passing through my mind. *Plant your feet, face your enemy, land the first punch, hit from the shoulders straight ahead, no roundhouse throws, thrust your body forward with the punch, and keep your right hand up in front of your face to take the counterpunch.* "Most fights end after one or two hits," Mike had said as I wiped the tears from my eyes after he demonstrated with a short jab to my vulnerable nose.

"What ya gonna do, Armpit?" Gordon taunted.

My fist struck Gordon square in the nose. He fell back on the wall, a thin trail of blood dripping from his nose. His eyes teared. I had to reach up to grab his neck, a haze of red anger clouding my vision.

"Go get my damn mitt, Gordon, or you'll be getting a face full of fists," I said.

Gordon wiped the blood from his nose, staring at it in studied disbelief as if the blood belonged to another. Gordon had never been hit for his mischief.

"OK, OK, I'll get it now, Armstrong," Gordon almost shouted. He hurried away, then returned quickly, mitt in hand. Lynn was watching from the shadow of the classroom door.

"Good punch, Jack. Where'd you learn that?" she asked.

"My brothers and friends box in the garage. I'm the youngest and usually the one getting punched," I remarked.

"I'd like to fight, Jack. How about you and me going at it after school?" she asked.

"Why don't you go fight some tough girl instead, Lynn?" I replied.

"Aw, they're so lame. Nancy gave up after I just knocked her on the ground," she said with a hand on her hip.

Lynn was easily the toughest girl in school. Vetal Elementary School straddled two distinct Detroit social networks. On the west side were tree-lined, middle-class neighborhoods with trim lawns and functioning street lights. On the east was a working-class, rough-and-tumble neighborhood, front yards as likely to be occupied by a car that needed to be fixed up as by a manicured lawn. Lynn and Gordon grew up east while I safely walked the streets west. Fighting Lynn was a no-win for me. If I was lucky enough to land the first punch and take her down, the guys would all joke that I just bested a girl. If she took me out, I would never live down losing to a girl.

"No, Lynn, I'm not going to fight you," I mumbled, as I walked away down the hall.

A week passed; then one Monday morning Lynn turned partly sideways and whispered, "They're after you, Jack."

In profile, Lynn was attractive, with dark brown eyes, short but soft black hair, and a fine, straight, Italian nose. At ten, I could observe these features but feel no arousal.

"Who's after me, Lynn?" I asked.

"Jimmy Hill and his gang," she replied.

"Why on earth would Jimmy Hill care about me?" I asked. Jimmy Hill was the toughest fighter in Vetal. Having somehow failed third grade, Jimmy was a year older and a mile tougher than the rest of us. His gang consisted of his older brother, Vince, and his friend, Lou. Lou, like Lynn, was Italian and liked to think of himself as the second toughest guy in school.

"He heard about your one-punch takedown of Gordon last week," she replied. "Some people are saying you're the toughest guy in school. Jimmy Hill doesn't like that idea. They'll be waiting for you after school. And Lou will be there with his knife, just in case you get Jimmy first."

"A knife!" I exclaimed. "Jimmy Hill and Lou with a knife. Oh my God!"

"Look for Terry in the circle when everyone knows there's going to be a fight. This is big, Jack!" Lynn exclaimed.

Terry Ontario was my biking friend. Terry and I also collected metal toy soldiers and Tonka trucks. But Terry was an unlikely fight ally, being overweight, out of shape, garrulous, nonathletic, and confrontation adverse.

"How is Terry watching in the crowd going to help me?" I asked.

"He'll step to the side and for a few seconds there will be an opening for a get away," said Lynn.

"You mean, run?" I gasped.

"You bet!" Lynn replied.

Running was not a fight strategy my brothers taught, but on reflection seemed like a good idea.

Upon exiting the school at 4 p.m., Jimmy Hill was easy to spot. Although only a year older, Jimmy could have been a ninth grader, with muscular, nonboy-like arms under a tight, black t-shirt and a face dominated by a wide, unsmiling mouth and piercing dark eyes. Jimmy was flanked by his even larger brother, Vince, and Lou, the knife boy.

"Let's go, Armpit," said Jimmy, as he pushed me with his right hand against my chest.

"I don't think so, Jimmy. Why don't you just hit me and I'll fall down and we'll call you the winner," I offered.

He pushed my chest again. "No, Jack, that's no fight. We'll do the real thing!" he retorted.

I looked to my right as I bounced back from Jimmy's chest shove. There in the circle of onlookers was unobtrusive Terry. He took a step to the side, creating a small opening in the circle of onlookers. I bolted through the gap, sprinting the next three blocks. As I slowed, the idea dawned on me that now I might be perceived as a coward. Cowardice would not be well received at home. A block away I spotted Dwight walking slowly toward our homes four blocks ahead. Dwight was two years older, tall and broad and wearing the white cross belt of the safety patrol.

"Hey, Jack, what's the hurry?" asked Dwight as I jogged up to him.

I explained to Dwight the circumstances of my rapid exit from the Jimmy Hill fight.

Dwight looked toward Vetal. "Look who's coming down the road, Jack, it's Lou," Dwight observed. Lou dismounted from his bike. He was thin, wiry, with a mean, weasel-like face.

"You thought you'd run away, Armweak," said Lou as he pulled his knife out and extended the thin steel blade.

"Whoa, this is between you two guys," said Dwight as he stepped aside. Lou took a step forward, his arm extended under-handed, his eyes fixed on mine.

I stood still, quiet, watching. Dwight quickly slipped behind Lou, pinned his arms to his sides, and knocked the knife from his hand. Dwight kicked the knife to the grass at the edge of the sidewalk.

"All right then, now it's just between the two of you. A fair fight," Dwight said as he stepped off the sidewalk and planted his foot over the open knife.

I now met Lou's gaze directly. He hadn't assumed a fighting stance. His arms hung from his sides. I took a step toward Lou and raised my fists into the fighting position my brothers had taught me.

"Let's go Lou," I said.

Lou looked at his knife beneath Dwight's foot, then at Dwight, and finally at me. "You think you're so tough. Wait till tomorrow with Jimmy, tough guy," Lou hissed.

Dwight reached down and handed me Lou's knife. "You might need this tomorrow, Jack," Dwight commented.

Lou backed up quickly, mounted his bike, and rode back toward Vetal.

Dwight and I walked slowly home, nothing left to say but "Thanks, man."

I debated telling my parents and brothers what had happened, but still not sure if I was smart, lucky, or a coward, I remained silent and sleepless.

The next day as I closed the hall locker, Jimmy Hill approached, alone. He smiled slightly. I felt the knife in my pocket.

"Hey, Armstrong. I heard about Lou and you last night. He backed down, huh?" Jimmy lightly punched my shoulder.

KNIFE

"He didn't want a fair fight, Jimmy," I said. "You and I don't have a problem, right? You're the King."

"Yeah, I'm the King. Don't you forget about that, Armstrong! You're OK!" Jimmy said, then turned and sauntered down the hall.

When I left Vetal to move to the countryside the next year, my classmates signed a note wishing me well. Lynn signed the note with a picture of a sharp pencil and a good luck wish. Lynn was my good luck.

I THOUGHT YOU WERE ALONE

A quiet, intense man, Dad sat in front of me at the breakfast table on assignment from my mother.

"So you want to be a doctor?" he started.

"I think I'll enroll in pre-med in the fall," I countered.

"We don't have any doctors in the family, and you don't know anything about doctoring or what a hospital is like." A matter-of-fact engineer, Dad liked to start conversations with a statement of facts.

"I guess I'll learn in time, Dad," I replied.

"What kind of work are you doing this summer?" he asked emphatically. Dad held a dim view of summer vacations. As he worked hard, he figured his son should, too. Once I had suggested summer hockey camp and within one week I had a demanding job painting Pontiac Grand Ams on the night shift assembly line.

"Not sure yet, Dad."

"There's a job as an orderly at Beaumont Hospital in Birmingham available next week. Here's the number to call." He got up to leave, paternal duty fulfilled.

I THOUGHT YOU WERE ALONE

Soon I was employed as a night orderly at Beaumont Hospital in Birmingham, Michigan, a prosperous, midwestern town. The hospital was easy to reach, just a thirty-minute drive down wide, four lane Woodward Avenue, flanked by suburbs. I drove to work each night in my Mom's white Corvair (unsafe at any speed) with a four-speed manual transmission and infamous rear engine. At night in the hospital I learned that the women prevailed. Most of the male doctors were either home, in the Emergency Department, or working late in the operating room. Sometimes I was assigned to Surgical Prep where a friendly group of six middle-aged women meticulously prepared the surgical packs for the next day's surgery. They liked teaching me about the packs, but laughed when I untied their aprons or sang Elvis songs while we worked.

Occasionally I was called to the medical wards to assist the beleaguered nurses, often with agitated, older men. One night I was called up STAT (like right now!) to find a small, young nurse attempting to calm a large, older man who was pacing the hall, his gown open in the back to reveal his generous bare bottom. As he strode back and forth he would periodically shout, "Help!" or "What's that?" The nurse explained to me that the man was going through DTs, or delirium tremors, from alcohol withdrawal and needed to return to his room where she could safely sedate him. I approached the old guy, known only as Mr. Brad, and asked him what the problem was.

"You don't see them? Don't tell me you don't see them?" he asked.

"Yeah, Mr. Brad, I think I do. But what do you see?"

"Bugs, son. Bugs on the walls, some on the floors, more flying around me." He swatted the air and stamped his feet at the same time. His hands trembled and his face twitched, but he wasn't really angry, just upset.

"You know, between us, I bet we could catch most of these bugs, then scoop them up and throw them out the window in your room," I said.

"You think? And you'd help me?" He now looked directly at me, both twitching eyebrows arched. This was my first lesson that to understand a delusion you have to join it for a while.

We grabbed the air and swiped at the walls. I put an arm around his shoulder and we staggered our way back to his room. The smiling nurse opened the window and we emptied our hands into the warm summer night. After standing at the window a few moments, Mr Brad sighed, then laid back on his bed.

"We'll call you again, Jack," said the nurse.

"Who do you usually call?" I asked.

"Generally Buck, the regular evening orderly, but he's busy in the ER with a really wild guy. Have you met him?" she asked.

"No, but I hear he's good."

"Yeah, good, but real quiet and tough. He was a prisoner of war for over a year in Korea. Not a man to cross," she replied.

One Friday night, my mom needed the Corvair for a girls' night out. Dad's new Impala was not then or ever available. I thought perhaps I'd miss a night's work, maybe even enjoy a summer date.

"I'll drop you off at the hospital. You can find a ride home." Dad didn't expect or tolerate opposing views.

On a late-night coffee break, I sat down at a table with Buck, who was sitting alone drinking black coffee. He was my height at 5'10," and 180 pounds of solid muscle. He wore a white t-shirt under green scrubs. His face was lined and serious as he nodded to me when I sat down. We ate donuts and sipped coffee for awhile; I was used to strong, silent men. My Dad and brothers never minded quiet and considered conversation during hockey or football games as odd.

Finally, I offered an opening. "Busy night."

"The usual," he replied.

"I heard you were in the service?" I asked.

"Army."

"Korea?"

"Yup."

"How was it?"

"Terrible, Kid. Don't talk about it much."

"Did you learn anything over there, Buck?"

He thought for awhile. "Yeah, one thing Kid: never show fear. They feed on it. Make them think you can always come at 'em."

"Think I could get a ride home tonight?"

"Where to?"

"Bloomfield Hills. On Gilbert Lake."

"Stomping in the high cotton, kid. But yeah, sure, come get me at eleven."

Eleven came around quickly, and we walked out to Buck's immaculate old Buick. The chrome sparkled. Buck rubbed a faint smudge off the deep blue hood. We drove out onto Woodward Avenue. Traffic was light and the night dark, without a moon.

About halfway home two motorcycles passed us and two more pulled in behind us. The lead biker slowed, then pulled us over to the side of the road. The riders dismounted and ambled over to the driver's side window. I sensed real danger.

The riders were 1950 hoods. They had long dark hair slicked back with hair oil. They each sported black leather jackets, tight jeans and a condescending scowl. Buck rolled the window down.

"Nice car, old man," said the lead hood. Buck reached underneath the dash and pulled out a large, loaded service revolver. He rested the pistol on his outstretched arm, now pointed at the lead hood's face. The big Buick engine purred in the quiet night.

The hood stared at the revolver, then at Buck, and said, "I'm sorry man, I thought you were alone."

Buck kept the revolver aimed at the hood's head as he sauntered back to his bike, started the engine and drove off.

We didn't talk the rest of the way home. I thanked him for the ride and wondered if a doctor's life would always be so dramatic.

A DETROIT MAN

Fall 1963 was crisp and beautiful at Miami University in Oxford, Ohio. Vietnam was a distant worry. The campus was alive with color from old trees, red brick traditional buildings, and the natural energy of youth.

I bunked in a small, two-man room in Anderson Hall, a freshman dorm. Friends developed quickly in the tight living quarters, each boy-man struggling to find a new, independent identity, yet not fail classes.

At the end of the hall lived Bill, a short, energetic, redheaded extravert, a high school track star with an idea a minute. We shared a trackman's past as well as a lust for adventure. Bill grew up in Chicago, so when the Miami University v. Northwestern football game arrived, he proposed a trip north to see the game and share blind dates par excellence. Big Gage, who lived at the far end of the hall, agreed to go as well on a rare, free weekend. Gage was as thick and huge as Bill was short and wiry. Gage threw the shot put for the track team, got all A's, and had a dry, slow sense of humor. You got the feeling talking with Gage that although he could crush a car, he would rather clean and pet it.

The drive to Chicago lasted five hours. Typical midwestern guys, we talked sports and high school exploits. Bill was especially interested in Detroit, a fighting man's town. I'd played hockey and football and had had my share of minor scraps. Neither Bill nor Gage ever had a serious fight. Not one to miss a chance to embellish a story, small fights retold became main events. The time passed quickly.

The hopeful Miami threesome met the Northwestern beauties at the tailgate party.

"Oh, my God, I think I've gone to heaven and an angel awaits me," Gage slowly exuded.

The beauties were indeed beautiful and excited about the game and the party afterwards. Christine, my date, was blonde, too attractive for a blind date, fully shaped, and had an easy laugh and good nature.

The football game was close and exciting. We drove happily together to the post-game party. The music was sixties rock, loud and driving. The beer flowed and the crowd was packed. We danced, laughed, sang, and the night pulsed away. During a slow dance, Christine leaned close, put her arms around my neck, and moved rhythmically with the music. As the song wound down, she whispered, "I have to slip away for awhile. I'll be back soon."

I danced with other girls, talked, and circulated the party for a while. Bill had also parted from his date; I spotted him in a corner engaged in a serious conversation with two guys I didn't recognize. Gage was in the middle of the dance floor doing the pony with the contorted, foolish smile of a thoroughly drunk, nineteen-year-old, lovesick guy. Christine was partially visible across the dance floor, arguing vigorously with a muscular, short-haired guy in a white t-shirt, who wore an aggrieved look on his face.

Bill, agitated, pulled me to a corner. "We're in deep trouble, Jack. Christine just broke up with her boyfriend, that big rock she's arguing with, and he and his buddies want a piece of all three of us!"

"Great, Bill, that's just great. Did you know all this before you set up the dates?"

"No, Jack. Really man, I didn't know a thing; but look, I got a plan. I told these guys about you, about Detroit, the fights and that you hurt some guys real bad."

"Are you crazy, Bill? That was high school and this is Chicago! And all three of these guys are big and mad."

"Yea, I know, Jack. Calm down, man. If things get out of hand, we got the Gage monster."

"Bill, look at Gage. See that goofy smile? That smile is twelve beers and a lot of you know what. He's useless unless he falls on top of them. Where are the girls?"

"Ah, see, they're a bit shook up and feeling guilty about the whole thing. They're waiting outside, just beyond that black door."

"You mean the door with the three short-haired goons lined up?"

"We got to walk out now, Jack. Look mean and tough. They think you're dangerous. I'll go first, Gage second, and you last."

We moved slowly toward the door and approached the Chicago lineup. Buck's maxim, "show no fear," faintly coursed through my mind.

Time seemed suspended and a low hum filtered through my mind, urging me to be silent and brave. Bill walked quickly by the three men and out the door. Gage ambled by, looking down his long, boney nose at each guy, then he too headed to the door, but stopped and waited. As I faced Christine's boyfriend, the last in line, I stopped and looked directly into his eyes. My jaw clenched slightly. The room was quiet. The aggrieved man stared back, but only for a few moments. The Chicago man broke his gaze, stared down, then to the left. I waited a second, then slowly walked out the door, Gage closing the door behind us.

We walked to the car and the waiting beauties.

"Oh, my God, I'm so sorry!" Christine exclaimed as she reached for my hand. "What happened?"

Gage and Phil looked at me.

"He looked away, Christine, so we walked out."

"You're kidding! He never backs down. I can't believe this!"

As we flowed into the car, Phil was unable to stop talking about our great escape. Gage leaned back and closed his eyes. Christine rested her head on my shoulder and her now warm hand cradled mine. My mind cleared, time resumed, and it was hard not to smile.

HERO

D r. Robbin Fleming slowly rose, pushed his chair carefully under the table, and studiously gazed at his assembled colleagues. All leaders and scholars, many were also his friends, yet tonight they were far apart. As University of Michigan president, Dr. Fleming encouraged open discussion, but now needed consensus. In 1968, most of the academic faculty opposed the Vietnam War and were vocally in favor of the anticipated student demonstrations. The alumni representatives were both World War II veterans and were disturbed that students would not support the war effort of their own government against the nefarious communists. The administrative leaders were concerned about order; the university must appear in control. But order was difficult at best to maintain in 1968. Earlier, both Martin Luther King and Robert Kennedy had been assassinated, and racial riots had rocked Detroit the previous summer. All present were alarmed that the Ann Arbor mayor had called for support from the National Guard to line the street and quadrangle adjacent to the Presidential Mansion.

HERO

President Fleming was middle-aged, intelligent, alert, and clearly in charge. A trained labor negotiator, he was adept at gradually coming to and coordinating agreement from disparate factions. Patience and reason were his allies.

"We've agreed then that we will permit the peaceful student demonstrations against the Vietnam War tomorrow night. The faculty," he said, nodding at the faculty chairman and vice-chairman, "may publicly express their views on the war and demonstrations, but not take part physically. The police and National Guard will keep order," he said, his eyes shifting to the Chief of Campus Police, who looked both anxious and dyspeptic, "but avoid direct contact with the students. All those in agreement raise their hands."

No one spoke or moved, but a few shifted in their chairs. Compromise always left everyone a little unsatisfied. Finally the faculty chairman, then the administrators, raised their hands, followed reluctantly by the rest of the group. Dr. Fleming smiled and nodded approvingly. He was a reasonable man. What could go wrong? As a parting comment, the Chief of the Campus Police pointed out that the National Guard was not under his authority.

Across campus, Malcolm sat down slowly in his chair, having just finished a passionate antiwar speech while urging nonviolence in the spirit of Martin Luther King. Malcolm was tall, black, and young, with long hair, dressed in jeans, a t-shirt, and horn-rimmed glasses. Malcolm was a graduate student and scholar as well as a member of the Black Panthers. Unlike most of his colleagues, he had witnessed violence up close and personal in Mississippi during racial protests. He knew the students were always the ones hurt. He agreed the protests were vital, but he also knew both the police and National Guard were being called out, which raised the risks for confrontation.

Gail rose next to castigate the capitalist pigs and their henchmen, the National Guard. Gail was dark haired, white, strikingly attractive, with fierce green eyes and a full figure daringly outlined by her tight t-shirt and jeans. As an economics major, she viewed the war and life as a materialist struggle of the people versus the powerful. She questioned if the Black Panthers were really black pussies, afraid of physical contact. After all, she reasoned, if there was violence, the press would be close behind and the antiwar movement needed exposure. Gail was an ardent Marxist who considered Stalin an aberration of a just ideology. She liked to refer to the triumph of her perspective as historically inevitable. Gail's only exposure to violence was when her Connecticut lawyer father spanked the dog for an untimely accident.

The National Guard Headquarters was off campus and dated back to the thirties. The lead guard, Major Dennis, was in full uniform. Dennis was fit, tough, white, and hardened by combat. Recently returned from a Vietnam tour of duty, he was committed to winning the war. He had witnessed firsthand the militancy of the Viet Cong and the unfortunate fate of the South Vietnamese villages that resisted Communist pacification. His impatience with student demonstrations was visceral, and he often stated to subordinates that the naive students needed to be taught a lesson. He had two hundred troops to line South University Avenue, which passed by the old, stately main campus as well as the dignified Presidential Manson. Against the advice of his two young lieutenants, Dennis had ordered full combat dress, including fixed bayonets in case the demonstrations turned into a riot. His lieutenants were younger, recent students, and had no experience with either combat or violence— they were horrified by the idea of shooting or bayonetting University of Michigan students.

The Peon was the new student newspaper of the University of Michigan Medical School. Although the small editorial staff was, in general, against the Vietnam War, they were mostly preoccupied with the many real demands of learning all that was required to pass National Board Examinations. Study nights lasted until midnight, and morning laboratory work was often demanding. I was the new Peon editor and asked for a volunteer to cover the demonstrations. John, the assistant editor, mentioned a rumor that some of the protesters were looking for a fight.

"And by the way," he said, "I have an actual date, a little joy for a tired and sequestered med student."

HERO

The remainder of the staff thought the editor should go and tell us all about it. I agreed to go, and my young wife, Jean, thought it might be interesting to break out of their workaholic routine.

My previous assignment covering a big campus event had been a disappointment. The noted author, Ken Kesey, of *One Flew Over the Cuckoo's Nest* fame, had given a speech at the University Undergraduate Student Union. Unfortunately, instead of discussing his brilliant novel, he read from the I-Ching while stoned and incoherent. We left quickly when they spotted drugs freely circulated among the equally stoned students.

Demonstration night was clear, and the students tried out a few chants as if we were at a football game. Unlike the Student Union crowd, no one was drunk or stoned. The National Guard was lined up across the courtyard, looking out of place in full uniform, helmets, and rifles. Gail stepped up to lead a chant, "Hell no, we won't go!" and the student mass wobbled forward like shaken jello. The soldiers held their ground.

Malcolm was at the front of the student body; he leaned left then right, urging his friends to stay cool. Dennis, now only ten yards from the taunting students, gripped his rifle and leaned toward his lieutenants and stated, "Be ready. We will not give way."

Dr. Fleming peered out his elegant window as the students approached the guards. He felt intense unease. He knew in his negotiator's gut that this was not going well. With each step forward by the students, the chance for violence escalated. He turned quickly to his wife and said, "This doesn't look good. I'm going out!" She sighed and reminded him his only useful weapon was his voice. He put on his coat and headed out the door.

To Malcolm's surprise, Gail and her three friends had brought ripe tomatoes to the demonstration. They stepped forward and yelled, "Pigs go home," and threw the tomatoes into the faces of the tense, young troops.

Dennis leaned over to his lieutenant on the right and ordered, "Let 'em have it!" The lieutenant released the tear gas canisters at the protesters just as Dr. Fleming crossed into the thin space separating the demonstrators and soldiers. Two quick breaths and the President collapsed.

The demonstrators and soldiers both came to a halt and fell silent. "Oh, no, not Dr. Fleming," said Malcolm. Malcolm, Gail, and Dennis reached Dr. Fleming together; he was breathing heavily and coughing. Dennis waved for the medics who hurried forward with a stretcher and oxygen. Malcolm and Gail motioned for the demonstrators to back away, then for everyone to go home. Dennis's two lieutenants moved the troops back.

The Ann Arbor News criticized the University administration for allowing the demonstration. *The Michigan Daily* criticized Dr. Fleming as being a weak supporter of the antiwar effort.

In 1968, no shots were fired, no student or soldier was injured, because one man, Dr. Robbin Fleming, a hero, stepped forward.

LUNAR NIGHTS

The site of the worst race riots during the sixties, Motown, the Motor City, home of the Lions and Tigers—Detroit was all these and more in 1970. Wide-spread illicit drug use, the sexual revolution, and the Vietnam War had unnerved the population. The city emergency room was often the only nocturnal safe haven for the injured, ill, and disoriented.

Ben was the surgical intern, and I was the medical intern assigned to staff the Detroit Wayne County Emergency Room. Wayne County Hospital was a 700-bed acute care hospital surrounded by a U-shaped, 2000-bed chronic psychiatric hospital. We reported for duty at 6 p.m. from Ann Arbor, home of the University of Michigan Medical School, to work a twelve-hour night shift. Bev, the head ER nurse, had warned us that tonight was a full-moon night and to expect the strange and unpredictable. Bev was a strong, wise, and practical nurse in her mid-forties who wore a slight frown or a thin smile depending on how chaotic things became and if we could control them. Her full moon superstition was shared by the entire ER staff, regardless of race, gender, or age. From her point of view, our job was to diagnose, treat, and comfort every patient who graced our doors no matter what circumstance had propelled them to us or what phase of the moon beamed down on us.

Ben, on the other hand, was a former college football player, intelligent, good natured, obsessive, and religious. He had short brown hair, a wide smile, a certainty that everything could be ordered if understood, and a total disbelief in the lunar myth. This was the first ER rotation for both Ben and me.

When I arrived in the ER at 6 p.m., the examination rooms were full of sick patients. Moans of pain, retching, and screams of distress overlaid the purring of the cardiac monitors and the soft conversations of nurses and patients. I worked ninety minutes straight before Bev, a slight frown on her pale, long face, informed me that Ben was late, and Ben was never late. Ben was punctual and neat, his small work area always orderly. I was unable to resist moving Ben's pen or file to the other side of the desk to enjoy his studied evaluation of the small permutation and changed space—then his careful movement of things back to their original order.

After 8 p.m. Ben appeared, looking more like a trauma patient than a physician. Ben slumped into his chair, spread his large arms and hands wide, and related his vexing tale.

"I was driving along I-96, on time to arrive at 5:45. I noticed a car pulled over on the shoulder of the road, a white rag tied to the door handle, flying in the wind. A young, good-looking woman stood beside the car and waved frantically for me to stop. I pulled over, got out of my car, and walked over. It was twilight, and the sun was fading as the huge full moon rose from the horizon. She told me the engine had made a loud knocking noise, then ground to a halt. She was upset, late for work, and asked if she popped the hood, would I take a look. Just as I leaned over the engine, two big guys appeared from the other side of the car, and one hit me with a bat and knocked me to the ground. They told me not to move, took my wallet, then hopped in the car with the girl and sped away. For a while I just laid on the gravel, my head hurting too much to move. Finally, I was spotted by a passing cop who pulled over, called an ambulance, and helped me up. I refused to go to the hospital, telling the medics I was headed here anyway. The cop said I was lucky I didn't fight back, or they might have killed me. After the medics cleared me, the cop followed me here to be sure I made it. Man, who would have thought I'd receive a good Samaritan's penalty. As the cop drove off, he pointed at the rising moon and shook his head."

I examined Ben, who was bruised and battered, but neurologically intact. He washed up and changed into green surgical scrubs. As Ben entered the first surgical room, he turned to Bev and said, "Well, I'm glad I've got my lunar curse over early!" Bev sighed and frowned but didn't reply.

After several steady hours of routine work—chest pains, the great flux, rashes, painful pee, and twisted ankles—traffic slowed, and Bev, Ben, and I collapsed in our steel back chairs to enjoy some strong coffee. The front desk secretary broke our quiet with a yell back, "Overdose en route. Arrival two minutes."

Bev punched my shoulder and said, "That's you, medicine man."

All kinds of drugs were circulating in the seventies, but amphetamines, LSD, and PCP (angel dust) were common and difficult to manage because of extreme patient agitation. Heroin overdoses were confined to regular users, only later to reach into all classes with the explosion in pain prescriptions. Hallucinogenic drugs were especially common in young, well-educated kids looking for visions, insight, and "Hey man, something new and wild."

The medics rolled in the gurney from the ambulance holding a raging, psychotic young woman restrained by arm and leg straps. Bev stepped up to accompany the medics to the exam room to place the cardiac monitor leads on her chest and to help the patient into her exam gown.

With a slight smile Bev said, "Give me just a minute, Dr. Armstrong, and this one is yours." I walked to our cramped work area with one of the medics who explained to me that the woman's roommate had related that they had shared LSD together, but the patient had taken an extra dose "to really get it on." As he finished his brief history, a blood-curdling scream pierced the air, and the young woman appeared outside the exam room, eyes wide, mouth open, completely naked. Bev and one big medic were right behind her, arms outstretched. Just as their arms approached the wild woman she bolted down the hall, passing Ben, a medic, and me as if we were frozen ice statues. She rounded the hall corner at full sprint, passing the desk receptionist, security guard, and two medics, and raced out the ER door heading straight for the hospital lawn leading to busy I-96. Ben and I exchanged quick glances and took off after her. Ben reached the naked woman first about fifty yards from the busy expressway. He made a perfect ankle tackle, but struggled to keep her under control. She screamed, "Pigs, let me go! Ah ya, ya, ya! They're coming after me! Look, look!" She pointed back at the hospital, then began beating Ben furiously with both fists. The moon above us was now full and bright.

Ben looked up at me and said, "I think this is a medical patient, Jack!" He lifted her up from the ground and onto my shoulder, quickly tying her ankles together with a phlebotomy tourniquet. She slowly turned her head to me, stared into my eyes and said, "Blue, the devil's eyes are blue," then spit on my forehead and kicked my back. The middle-aged Hispanic security guard finally arrived, draped a brown blanket over the struggling young woman, and we began our march back to the ER.

"Oh no, oh no. They're coming for me. Help, help!" she screamed. I looked into her large, very-dilated brown eyes.

"Who is after you?" I asked.

"The panthers. The black, lean, hungry panthers. Oh, God, no, no, leave her alone!" she pleaded.

"Are they chasing you?"

"They're chasing a small lamb and oh, oh, the lamb has turned to us and its face is my face! Save it!"

"Why are the black panthers after the lamb?"

"They want to catch her and tear her apart. Oh, no, no, they're getting closer!"

"Imagine yourself as the lamb. Try to get inside her . . . Are you there?"

"I'm there. OK, but I'm so afraid!"

"Now roar. Roar like a lion, like you're not afraid, but ready to fight back," I paused while she roared into the night. "What happened?"

"They stopped! The panthers are backing away!"

"What's your name, little lamb?"

"Sarah. Sarah Bentley. You're a nice doctor, will you take me back to the hospital now?"

"That's where we're headed, Sarah Bentley. Are you a student?"

"Yeah, I'm a psych major at Wayne State. Oh, oh. . . they're still looking at me, and their jaws are open and dripping blood. Oh, what have they killed? Help! Help me!"

"Roar, Sarah! Roar like your life depended on it."

"Arrrrrrrrrrrrrrrrrrrrrr!"

"What's happening?"

"They're backing off. I think they might go looking for another lamb."

"We're almost back to the ER now. The nurse will give you a gown, and I'll give you some medication to calm you down until the psychiatrist arrives."

"Your voice is so calm. I think I'm getting sleepy already. I took the LSD to know what they were seeing."

"Who was seeing?"

"The patients. The psych patients we've been reading about. The hallucinations of the mad."

"Now you know."

"Oh, God, what was I thinking? Oh, ouch. Egads!"

"What happened?"

"Electric shocks just came out of the sky and are piercing my head. Pain, pain."

"Do you see the rock in front of you?"

"Yes, I see it. Oh, the lightning is burning my hair!"

"Pick up the rock and hold it over your head and the shocks will bounce off."

Sarah's arms reached over her head holding the imaginary rock, then held steady.

"Well?"

"The shocks are bouncing off. The pain is going away."

"We're here now, Sarah. I'm placing you on the stretcher. Keep your arms over your head. I'll see you soon."

Sarah was only nineteen. She was admitted to the hospital psychiatric service for five days. The terrifying hallucinations slowly receded. The psychiatrist remarked that her lion roars could be heard in downtown Detroit. As Sarah was rolled to the elevator to the psychiatry ward, an orthopedic patient was brought back for Ben's attention.

"You won't believe this," Ben stated, looking incredulously at Bev and me. "Orthopedics. What is more straightforward than bones and joints? A cast here, a brace there, it's fractured or it's sprained. But this next patient has two broken tibias, both fractured in the same place? How could that happen? I asked the patient to explain this as I was placing him in traction and waiting for the on-call orthopedic surgeon."

The patient hung his head and replied. "My wife said, 'Don't do it. Just call the tree guy.' But I could see the cracked limb. I could reach it with my extension ladder. As I climbed up, I noticed the full moon, just behind the limb. I went into a trance, I think. I began to dream of the first time I took my wife out on a golf course with a blanket and a bottle of wine. We were so young and everything was so new. I climbed out on the limb, the saw in one hand. Somehow I could get a better grip by sitting on the limb. The moon was so bright, my wife so young, and her skin so soft. I sawed away and the limb cracked and fell, and I fell too, straight down and landed on both feet, twenty feet down. I guess I'm lucky it was just my legs."

Ben smiled and looked at Bev. "I guess that's the last of the lunar crazies?"

Bev reached for the phone at that moment. She listened for a while, her whole face turning into a frown.

"Just a minute, Sir, I have the doctor here. Let me see what he thinks." She punched the hold button. "You are not going to believe this. It could be a prank call, but the guy seems like he's in a real panic. Will you talk to him?"

"How could it be worse then what we've already seen?" I asked.

Bev punched the hold button and handed the phone to me.

"This is the Doctor," I said.

"We got trouble here, Doc," a man replied, breathing heavily. "Real trouble. I was making love to my girlfriend. We were really going at it. Then I was done, right, so I began to pull out, but I'm stuck. Every time I try to exit I seem to get caught, and she screams bloody murder. So we're lying here, see, and I don't know what to do."

"Don't try to come out again. Give the nurse your address and we'll send an ambulance out to bring you both in. Wrap up in a blanket and I'll see you soon."

Twenty minutes passed and the couple was brought back on the stretcher in the missionary position. The girl explained that they had been drinking a lot and looking at the full, radiant moon. Her boyfriend opened the window to let the moonlight in, and then they really went at it. When he was done he tried to withdraw, but each time it felt as if he was pulling her insides out.

The pelvic exam was difficult, with the boyfriend pushed to the side. The light illuminated her vagina and the man's uncircumcised penis could be seen ensnared with the laces from her intra-uterine device. Each time he moved, the captured penis tugged on the cervix, pulling the uterus forward. The cuts of the laces were tight, but eventually the man and the penis were free. The gynecology resident removed the IUD. The couple were grateful but embarrassed, and for some reason blamed the moonlight, not the IUD for their trial.

The night slowly wound down. Ben was in the surgical suite sewing up a forehead laceration of a young boy who had fallen off his new bike, which he had decided to ride in the driveway in the moonlight. Bev pushed the wheelchair occupied by a balding, middle-aged businessman in a tailored sports coat and red silk tie across from my desk. Bev's weary face now had a permanent frown, and her left eyelid twitched rhythmically.

Bev paused the wheelchair across from me and said, "He has chest pains, Doc. He said he's had crushing mid-sternal chest pain for an hour."

The businessman looked up from the wheelchair and said, "Look, Doc, I don't want to be here. What are you, just an intern? Jesus Christ, I told those damn medics to take me to my private hospital, but 'Oh no,' they said, 'You're having a heart attack, and we're taking you to the closest ER, Wayne County. Time is really important.' So here I am." His face was as white as the moon, and perspiration was apparent on his upper lip.

"What were you doing when the chest pain began?" I asked, noting the contrast between his Harris Tweed jacket and his dirt-stained hands.

He looked embarrassed and hesitated for a moment, but like most men whose lives are in the balance, decided to tell the truth.

"I woke up at 4 a.m. and couldn't go back to sleep. The moon was huge and shining through our bedroom window. I figured I might as well dress for work. I work for GM in Rochester. After I dressed, I looked out the window again, and the moonlight had illuminated the whole backyard, particularly the part I had been raking last night, but didn't finish. I'd left the wheelbarrow half full of leaves and those damn walnuts. So I thought, well, might as well finish the job. I loaded up the wheelbarrow and was pushing it up the hill to dump it in the mulch pile when it felt like a vise had grabbed my chest and was clamping shut. I became short of breath and broke out in a sweat. I made it back inside, and yelled to my wife to call the rescue squad. As we drove off in the squad car, you could see the whole yard lit up by the moon. Strange."

As the man said "strange," his voice trailed off. After a moment he began to tremble, then shake, and finally his arms and legs began to twitch in tonic clonic movements. Suspecting he was developing ventricular tachycardia during the acute ischemic stage of his heart attack, I leaned across the narrow work desk and hit him firmly in the sternum. An external cardiac thump had been known to cardiovert ventricular tachycardia. After a brief pause, the seizure stopped, he regained consciousness, and said, "Damn, Doc, that really hurt. Why'd you do that?"

Bev nodded at the cardiac room and rolled the stretcher quickly back. Rapidly we undressed him, slid the gown on, and placed the cardiac monitor leads. I slipped an intravenous catheter into his arm and Bev drew up the IV lidocaine. As we checked the monitor, his cardiac rhythm switched from rapid sinus tachycardia to ventricular fibrillation, a serious cardiac arrhythmia that cannot support blood pressure or life. His tonic clonic seizures resumed.

Bev wheeled the defibrillator to the bedside. I pushed the IV lidocaine through the new IV as Bev cranked up the voltage on the defibrillator.

"Ready to go, Doc," Bev said.

I placed the defibrillator pads on his chest, applied the paddles, and pressed the discharge switches. The defibrillator shocked the patient's chest, and he rose abruptly from the stretcher.

Ben had entered the room to help, as did two additional nurses. Ten eyes focused on the cardiac monitor. The seizures slowed, then stopped. The monitor displayed the normal rhythm and echoed the reassuring regular beeps.

"We need to get to the Coronary Care Unit quickly!" said Bev.

As we wheeled the stretcher through the exam room door leading to the elevator, the patient resumed groggy consciousness.

"Damn, my chest really hurts!" He focused on me, paused, then said, "I'm going to look for you, buddy, when this is over."

We wheeled him quickly through the ER, into the elevator, then into the Coronary Care Unit where expert hands took over.

Ben, Bev, and I sat quietly in our small, now-cluttered work area. Three untouched steaming cups of coffee and three large chocolate donuts rested in front of us. Ben's warm smile was gone, his hair was rumpled, and his hands rested in his lap. Bev no longer smiled or frowned, and her left eye twitched constantly. My insides were empty, spent. Bev looked up first to Ben, then to me, and said, "Just walked outside. It's dawn. The sun is rising. The moon has set. We should be OK now."

Ben and I both sighed, but neither of us corrected her.

Ten days later, at the night shift start, Bev poked her alert face around the corner, both eyes arched but not twitching, and said, "Someone here to see you, Doc."

A well dressed, balding, middle-aged businessman appeared around the corner, a serious expression on his face. Had he at last returned to even the score? A wide smile broke out on his face, and his hand extended to mine.

"Thank you, Doc, for a really good punch. I'm going home today!"

SPECIAL GIRLS DAY

The hospital doctor conference room at University of Michigan Hospital was a long, grey rectangle cluttered with patient medical charts and numerous paper laboratory slips. Electronic medical records and computers were decades away. A small conference table and a set of folding chairs occupied the room's center. A single window peered out onto a spring courtyard, permitting a thin ray of sunlight to reflect off the wall. The chalkboard was full of patient lists divided by student and intern responsibilities; the probable working diagnosis was handwritten under each name. The room was quiet. The overhead lights were off.

I reclined in one of the folding chairs, feet propped up on the table, eyes closed. My short white coat and starched white pants were crumpled and stained with sweat, patient urine, blood, and pocket ink. My tie was loose and my face carried a two-day beard. It was 5 p.m. on Monday afternoon, the end of a marathon weekend of hospital call rotation. Leaving our apartment at 7 a.m. Friday morning, I kissed Jean goodbye and promised to be home Monday night at 6 p.m. She promised a special spaghetti dinner.

Stan, the medical chief resident, opened the conference room door quietly and slipped into a chair next to me. Stan had served two years in the military after graduating from Harvard Medical School and now was completing his internal medicine training. We all considered Stan a genius and a control freak. He had a buzz cut, his long white coat was spotless, trousers pressed, tie centered, face freshly shaven, and nails trimmed. He shook my chair gently.

"OK, Jack, wake up now, time to check out. The other interns are tied up. Let's go through the cases. By the way, you look like shit. Have you been here all weekend?" he asked.

I stirred, blinked, and yawned. "Yeah, Stan, all weekend—Friday, Saturday, and Sunday nights. We had five code blues, twenty admissions, and forty-five patients to round on. The students were a big help." I yawned again.

"Son of a bitch, Jack, you never got home at all, not even for dinner! My wife would have been pissed! Where are the students?" he asked.

"Home, I sent them all home exhausted. Nobody slept over two hours last night," I replied.

Stan's speech was always a surprise. No coarse word or vulgarity was beyond him. When he spoke from his perfect military face and neat uniform, it was as if he were occupied by a foul, trash-talking alien.

"Jesus, man, let's go through the cases. I'll brief the other interns. You've set some sort of fucking record here, Jack!"

After reviewing the admissions, discharges, deaths, and active cases, Stan lead me into the hall. "Go, Jack. Get the fuck out of here, and don't think of us or the patients," he demanded.

It was 5:40 p.m. and there was still dinner with Jean. As I turned the corner to leave the patient wards, a harried nurse stuck her head out of a patient room and yelled, "Code Blue! We need you in here now, Jack!"

The room was full of students, nurses, and a respiratory therapist, but no doctor. We shifted into full throttle, but the middle-aged man on the hospital bed remained in ventricular fibrillation, a fatal heart arrhythmia—a moment from death. A big male medical student was performing vigorous chest compressions, and the respiratory therapist had the endotracheal tube in place with supplemental oxygen.

"We've tried IV epinephrine, lidocaine, bicarbonate, calcium, and three cardio-versions. What now?" the worried nurse asked.

"Do you have the intraventricular needle attached to the epinephrine vial?" I asked.

The nurse handed me a long intracardiac needle. I inserted the needle below the xiphod process and into the heart, injected the epi, then reshocked the man with maximum voltage. Stan stepped into the room.

"What the fuck, Jack! I sent you home! What are you doing here?" he exclaimed.

The young cardiac nurse stepped between me and Stan.

"I caught him in the hallway," she explained. "Only Doctor around."

"Is that a damn intracardiac needle, Jack?" he asked, his tone somewhere between awestruck and incredulous. "Did you inject the patient directly into the heart? Holy fucking cow! Did it work?"

The nurse pointed to the cardiac monitor. "Back in sinus rhythm, Dr. Leonard! We have a blood pressure."

Stan grabbed my shoulders and pushed me to the door. "Now, for God's sake go, Jack. Don't look left, don't look right, don't look back. Just get the hell out of here! I'll take charge," Stan instructed.

I finally left the hospital at 6:30 p.m., drove to Maiden Lane Apartments on the Huron River, and slowly opened the door to our small, two-bedroom apartment with a sense of foreboding. Jean was standing at the stove, the pasta boiling, the uncooked hamburger on the counter beside her right hand. Jean's father was a former college football player who wished for a son. Receiving two daughters, he took Jean, his oldest daughter, to the front yard after dinner for a game of catch. Jean could throw a perfect twenty-yard spiral, a feat I appreciated on our first date in a coed football game.

Jean reached for the big pound of hamburger and kneaded it into a football, turned, and fired the hamburger ball straight at my head. Fixed wearily at the door, I watched the hamburger spiral just over my head, strike and stick to the door for a moment, then plop to the floor. Jean started to cry.

I picked up the hamburger, walked over to her and kissed her tears. "I'm sorry, honey. Will you forgive me?"

"Yes, Dr. Late, I forgive you."

"Do you think we can still eat the spaghetti meat sauce?" I asked.

"You better, Jack, it's all we have!"

A medical intern is a haunted being caught in the chasm between student and responsible physician. Encapsulated for years in premedical, then medical education, the student is limited in time and space. There is never enough time to learn everything presented as necessary to be a physician. Having so little free time, the student's space circuit is confined to classrooms, lecture halls, the library, and perhaps the gym and an occasional bar. Somewhere in distant time looms the inevitable National Board Examination and, if passed, graduation into internship. There the patient materializes, a sick being often unsure of the source of his torment, desperate for an explanation or diagnosis, and perhaps relief or treatment.

The intern is in the front line trench, often the first to attempt to translate a diffuse history and difficult physical exam into a working diagnosis and plan. The intern's time cluttered with distractions, including the ubiquitous pager and phone, is intense. Suffering now lies directly in front of him, no longer an abstraction. Life outside these intense encounters fades. Politics, the best movies of the year, where the finest new restaurant is, or what you may think of the new Corvette slip away from lack of attention. Only the distant fire of Vietnam has the power to intrude, as most physicians in 1971 were auctioned off by the draft lottery to some form of government service. My draft number was a conspicuous single digit, a certain calling.

The Berry Plan offered a chance for a drafted doctor to upgrade to an officer in the Air Force as a flight surgeon, an exciting title implying air flight, adventure, and the dignity of surgery with wounded warriors. The weekend trial of 24-hour-call and sleepless nights temporarily over, I slumped into our old living room chair with my beautiful, dark-haired wife, Jean, and our black cat, Magic, settled on my lap.

"The Air Force called Saturday, while you were at the hospital and will call back at 8 p.m. sharp tonight," purred Jean.

"What did the great force of air want from me?" I asked.

Jean nestled into my neck then slowly licked my ear.

"Will you be awake at 8 p.m., Jack-Jack, to keep a poor girl company?" Jean whispered. She leaned her wonderful, soft chest into mine and ran her hand slowly through my hair. In spite of only two hours sleep, my whole body seemed to rise to attention.

"Before I lose my mind, honey, you better tell me what the great force of air wanted," I said.

Jean sighed and sat up slightly.

"Well, he wants to explain our assignment, just briefly to tell us what is going to happen to our whole fucking life for two years."

Magic purred as I rubbed her neck softly. Jean knew the assignment could take us away from Ann Arbor, our liberal enclave, to anywhere, perhaps even the furnace of Vietnam.

At 8 p.m. sharp dessert was interrupted by the phone ringing.

"Good evening, Dr. Armstrong. This is Colonel Johnson, U.S. Air Force."

"Sir, are you calling about our assignment?"

"Yes, Doctor. You will be joining the Air Force as a first Lieutenant Flight Surgeon and assigned to the Kansas City Induction Center."

"What will be my duties, sir?"

"Physical exams, Doc. Hundreds of induction physicals."

"Not Vietnam?"

"Probably not."

"But I'll be learning to fly, right, as a flight surgeon?"

Colonel Johnson snorted, then laughed. "No son, that flight surgeon term isn't a real thing. No, we leave the flying to the pilots. Physical exams, that's your job. Get the boys ready for basic training."

"How about surgery then, as in flight surgeon? You'll be training me as a surgeon, right?"

The Colonel laughed again. "You do have a good imagination, son, but no, no surgery either. Things are not as they appear or sound. You're a medical intern, son. We leave the surgery to the surgeons. Think of a long line of basically healthy young men eager to be soldiers and you either open the gate for them to be soldiers or pronounce them 4F and send them home."

As I replaced the phone, Jean slipped her arms over my shoulders, kissed my neck and said, "Think later, Jack, enjoy now." My troubled mind closed to the future as I felt warmth spread quickly, miraculously through my weary body.

Three weeks later a late night call rang again.

"Dr. Armstrong, this is Dr. Bates at the Army Research Laboratory at Fort Dietrich, Maryland, and I have an opportunity for you."

"Dr. Bates, I'm joining the Air Force in July, Sir, as a flight surgeon. Sort of."

"This job could replace the Induction Center in Kansas. You're a physician and a chemist and that's just what we need in our animal research facility in southern Mississippi."

"Southern Mississippi animal research. Doing what, Sir?"

"We're studying the neurological effects of a powerful new chemical called Agent Orange, a defoliant used extensively in Vietnam. Have you heard of it?" he asked.

Television news images of stripped landscapes and whole hills on fire passed quickly across my mind. "Yeah, Agent Orange.

I've heard about it, doing animal neurological research in southern Mississippi, this is very different."

"Think on it, Doctor. This is a real opportunity for an open mind," he concluded.

I put the phone down slowly and laid my head back to reflect. Magic curled on my lap, purring. Jean had already begun to cry. She rose from her chair and wagged a long, teacher's finger at my eyes. Jean read and watched the news after returning from teaching school and kept an alert eye on the erupting war and how it seemed to be growing like a malignant tumor.

"No, Jack. No, no, no. Don't even think about it! Agent Orange is an awful thing. Kills everything it touches, including you and all the rats that will surround you. And southern Mississippi? Oh, God. I'll die there too, a northern liberal woman surrounded by bleeding rednecks. Oh, why did I marry a doctor? My mother warned me to never marry a doctor!"

There would be no happy warmth tonight.

Two weeks and 150 stress-filled hours of work later, the phone rang a third time. Was there yet hope?

"Doctor Armstrong, this is Dr. Henderson at the Centers for Disease Control in Atlanta, Georgia. Do you know who we are?"

"Yes, sir. We all know of you. You are the biggest and best microbiology facility in the world."

"How would you like to work for us, Doc? We'll train you as an epidemiologist. This is science in action: the classroom, the lab, then the field, doing cutting edge work. A terrific opportunity!"

Hardly believing our good fortune, we went to Atlanta at the completion of the internship, moved into a spacious two-bedroom apartment, left dreary night call behind, and enrolled in the Epidemic Intelligence Service's (EIS) famous course in biostatistics and epidemiology. Epidemiology is the branch of medicine that deals with the incidence, patterns of distribution, and control of both acute and chronic diseases. Originally concerned with infectious diseases only, the CDC evolved into applying the statistical techniques to many chronic problems, including violent death and heart disease. Nevertheless, their excellence in teaching, figuring out, and controlling infectious disease outbreaks was unchallenged.

Jean went to work as a reading specialist. After finishing the EIS course, I was assigned to the Division of Sexually Transmitted Diseases, an area of increasing national concern because of rising incidence rates. Formally the Division of Venereal Diseases, the name had been changed to STD to remove the moral stigma of venial or minor sin.

In the seventies, before the arrival of the human immuno-deficiency virus (HIV) and the explosion of the acquired im-munodeficiency syndrome (AIDS) epidemic, we were concerned about simultaneous epidemics of gonorrhea, chlamydia, syphilis, and genital herpes. The division supervised numerous clinical and laboratory research studies to improve diagnosis and treatment, as well as explore new approaches to prevention. I was assigned studies to follow and oversee, often involving onsite travel, lectures to field teams, and meeting with research directors. After several months of training and active research, one of the lab-based EIS officers approached me about moonlighting one weekend in a north Georgia rural emergency room.

"You'll like it, Jack. Keep your clinical skills sharp. Easy to rust here at the mecca. But be prepared. The place is really remote. Just you and the nurses—mostly routine though. You can take my rotation to start off," Dick offered.

"No trauma or desperate babies who need to be intubated?" I questioned.

"Nah, nothing that exciting," he reassured me.

The drive to north Georgia was beautiful—hilly and rural. The hospital was small, only fifty beds, and an old ER. The nurses were actually just one experienced surgical nurse in her mid-for-ties named Elaine, who had signed on to work the whole weekend, and a young receptionist, Jan, who doubled as a phlebotomist.

The work pace was leisurely and the patients friendly and not too ill. Friday night slowed down and I even slept six hours. Sat-urday was busy but straightforward until a young nurse presented her ten-year-old son with a scalp laceration incurred by a headfirst dive into second base during a sandlot baseball game. Second base was a large rock. After cleaning up his wound, I asked the mom to step into the waiting room while I sutured the bloody scalp. The mother reassured me, as a surgical nurse, that blood did not bother her, and she preferred to stay with her son. Elaine's eyebrows arched, and she took the mother's arm to direct her to the lobby.

"Look, Elaine, let go of my arm. I need to stay with Bobby," the mother insisted.

Elaine sighed and opened the surgical pack. The boy was quiet. We cleaned up his wound and infiltrated the skin edges with a local anesthetic. Elaine handed me the sutures and needle, and I began to close the wound. The human scalp is vascular, and even the small opening created by the surgical needle led to bright red bleeding.

Elaine partially caught the mother as her eyes rolled back in her head, the blood drained from her face, and she fell backward, landing on the hard floor with a thud. A laceration appeared on the back of her scalp. After reviving the mother we cleaned up her scalp and closed the laceration. The mother willingly waited in the lobby while we finished closing Bobby's wound. The mother hugged us all, apologized for forcing her way into the surgical suite, and left with a promise to upgrade second base from a stone to a towel.

"Well, that should be our excitement for the night," said Elaine as we opened our package of doughnuts and sipped fresh coffee. After a brief pause the ER intercom crackled, "EMS on the way. Forty-year-old male, gunshot wound from his wife to the chest. Hypotension and hemorrhage. ETA four minutes."

We scrambled. The receptionist, Jan, paged our only surgeon, who was not onsite. Elaine and I ran to the surgical suite, found the chest tube and central line trays, and called the laboratory for blood and IV fluids. Too soon EMS burst through the doors, blood all over everyone, the lead EMS tech holding a surgical towel tight to the wound.

We rushed the large, semiconscious man onto the surgical table. The chest gunshot wound was deep, to the lung. No breath sounds could be heard over the left chest. We cleaned the chest wound quickly, infiltrated lidocaine, and rapidly inserted the chest tube with a dramatic release of blood and air. Next, we inserted intravenous lines in his arms and prepared to insert a large central line IV catheter into his left chest to administer a much needed blood transfusion. Elaine and I were focused on the task at hand, working directly on the desperate man, the world at large invisible and inaudible.

We heard but did not look up to see the steel doors from the reception area to the surgical suite burst open. Jan yelled out, "Wait, you can't go in there!"

The disheveled forty year old wife rushed through the doors. As we looked up she froze for an instant, her eyes wild with fear. We looked from her face to her hands, hoping the gun had been left behind. The wife wrestled free of Jan and ran across the suite to land on her knees at her delirious husband's wounded side, hands empty of a handgun.

"Oh, God, oh God, Harold, forgive me! I didn't mean for this to happen." The wife laid her head on Harold's arm just as Jan and the breathless general surgeon reached the bedside. Jan firmly but gently guided the distraught wife to the waiting room. The surgeon stepped forward and said, "Good work, son. Hemopneumothorax, right? Unstable and still bleeding. We need to go to OR now!" One minute later surgeon and patient disappeared down the OR corridor, both to emerge exhausted but alive hours later.

Sunday at 4 p.m. I handed over responsibility to the incoming ER doc; Elaine hugged me, smiled, and said, "I guess we won't be seeing you again, Doctor A. We did well, you and I!"

Back to the CDC I returned. All four STD epidemics continued to rage unabated. I met Dick Martin and Dwight Lane in the research microbiology laboratories. Dick was attempting to develop a more sensitive way to culture Neisseria gonorrhea using a candle jar to generate carbon dioxide to facilitate bacterial growth. Dr. Lane was chief of the Treponema (spiral bacteria that cause syphilis, yaws and pinta) research labs. He was attempting to develop a new florescent antibody serologic test to more accurately diagnose syphilis. Both men grumbled about the lack of fresh patient specimens to work with.

Sid plunged into the chair across from my desk. Sid was our division chief physician, a large man with a ruddy face, volatile temper, and a sterling training record in internal medicine and infectious diseases from the University of Washington in Seattle. Both brilliant and charismatic, Sid was a bundle of energy, ideas, and enthusiasm. "We have a problem, Jack, that I think you are perfectly suited to help us fix," he began.

"I thought I was doing fine right here, Sid," I offered, sensing trouble.

"Yes, yes, you are doing fine. But this is a new idea, a real opportunity, something that will help our colleagues in the lab, the people in Atlanta, and the STD division too. We need better STD diagnostic tests that are rapid, simple, and accurate. To do that, we need fresh clinical specimens. To get these specimens we need a new clinic in downtown Atlanta, in the midst of a poor neighborhood with the highest rate of syphilis and gonorrhea in the state, and no access to health care," he stated.

Sid bounded out of my chair, his face flushed with enthusiasm, and paced the small space in front of my desk.

"And you can do this, Jack! You can be the first Medical Director of the new clinic. You'll have the latest and the best medical equipment, as well as a full nursing and epidemiological staff. We will train you on how to do phase dark field microscopy so you can diagnose primary syphilis on the spot and meet the lab leadership in the field. Cutting edge, Jack."

Jean reluctantly dropped me off at the Marta train station in Decatur close to the CDC campus. We only had one car, which she needed in order to go to school to teach each morning. Her worry was the new clinic was located in the poorest and most violent part of Atlanta. The city was volatile in 1973; civil rights, crime, and integration of schools and hospitals were explosive issues. Andrew Young was a civil rights leader and new Democratic congressman from Georgia, later to become mayor in 1982; progressive Jimmy Carter was governor, and change was in the air. Grady Hospital, an enormous downtown city hospital affiliated with Emory University, had just integrated its patient wards, ending decades of separate black and white clinical towers.

The Marta train dropped me off blocks from the new clinic building. The streets became unpaved and were lined with small residential homes and apartment buildings. My clinic staff included six nurses: one white and five black. The epidemiological investigative staff was mostly black as well. All staff were native Georgians and proud of it. We had great equipment, including a phase microscope to allow direct visualization of live spirochetes as they tumbled across the dark field illuminated by bright light. The exam rooms were well outfitted and the small reception area was welcoming, like a private practice. We had all the tools to not only see patients, but also to obtain specimens, and to start several new clinic research projects.

One project entailed defining the microbiological causes of genital ulcers; another the relationship of sexual behavior to various types of sexually transmitted diseases.

After one week at the clinic I noticed that the five young black nurses were walking several blocks at twilight to the bus station to go home. I suggested to them one evening that this was risky and I would, as the only male present at 6 p.m., escort them to the bus station. My suggestion was initially met with broad smiles, then laughter.

"What's so funny?" I asked.

"Well, Doctor A.," said Jenny, the most attractive and the leader of the black nurses, "we're actually worried about you. Do you see any other white guys around here? And you are being watched," she replied.

Jenny was 5'6," with long dark hair, large brown eyes, a great figure only partially concealed by her conservative nurse's uniform. From a religious family, Jenny often hummed gospel hymns and could quote the Bible by verse.

"And who is watching me?" I asked.

"The brothers, Doc. All the young black men in this neighborhood. They don't know why you are here and what you are really up to. They don't trust white doctors, particularly after the Tuskegee study. So let's go, Doctor A., we girls are going to walk right down the middle of the street with you to the MARTA station."

"What is that going to prove, Jenny?" I asked.

Jenny's face now became serious. "That you are with us. One team. After that, they will watch you, but leave you alone," she replied.

So I left my manly pride in the clinic and walked slowly down the street among five casual, talkative, black nurses. Periodically, a black man appeared in an alley or window or would stop working on his car in his front yard to gaze at us. This lesson was not taught in the EIS course. All was well.

The following week Jenny came into my small, spare office at 8:30 a.m. before the 9 a.m. clinic began.

"This is an unusual clinic today, Doctor A. We call it 'Special Girls Day.'"

"What's so special about these girls, Jenny?" I asked.

"They are high-priced prostitutes, Doc, and two cops are bringing them here to be checked out and certified clean of STDs by you. All off the record of course," she replied.

"This must be a little shocking for you, Jenny, given your family's religious background."

Jenny laughed and patted my arm, "No, growing up black in Atlanta, nothing surprises me."

In my mind's eye, I imagined two upright and disapproving men of the law escorting six disheveled, somewhat shamefaced, unattractive, weary women into my clinic. Instead, two jovial young men in blue escorted six very attractive, well-dressed young women into our waiting room, everyone talking and joking, cops and women on a first-name basis.

Officer Joe stepped forward and handed me the paperwork, clearly not Fulton County or Federal documents.

"Appreciate you taking care of these gals, Doc. A good bunch. Be sure to sign and complete each form. Let's keep this little examination quiet though. The Feds and administrators tend to be a bit uptight, OK?" he asked.

"OK, Officer. No need for publicity. We'll take care of everything," I replied. There was a rumor that the local university used cash and prostitutes in their basketball and football recruiting. Were these the secret women?

The young ladies of the night were cooperative. No bruises or needle tracts were noted, findings which were common on exams of prostitutes in ERs. The last woman to be examined was tall and muscular. She sauntered into the exam room with a flirtatious smile and wave of her hand to the officers.

Jenny stepped forward and said, "I'll set her up for a pelvic exam. You come in in a few minutes."

Jenny's scream shot out and through the exam room door, bounced off all four walls of the reception room, and settled on my ears. The exam room door burst open, and Jenny stomped out shaking her finger at the patient.

"The doctor will be in to deal with you!" she exclaimed.

"Well?" I asked, a still-upset Jenny standing indignantly in front of me.

"She is not a she, but a he! I set her or him up for a pelvic exam, draped her, and pulled her pink panties down and there it was. A big, fat penis! I actually touched it, jumped back I was so startled, and ran right into the wall. And he laughed. He enjoyed the whole thing! What a pig."

I went into the pelvic room, chided him about his joke, and ensured his promise to apologize to Jenny. On exam he was very feminine but definitely a man of the night. After he was dressed and formally declared clean, I asked him how this worked, who it was that signed up for him?

"Oh, almost exclusively gay men still in hiding," he replied.

"But why the feminine disguise?" I asked.

"It's all part of the game. Most of the men are upright married men, secretly gay, with wives, family, and jobs. They enjoy the whole dress-up, make believe of meeting a secret woman, while what they really desire is another man. Believe me, Doc, it's not the weirdest thing I see."

"Very interesting, but you really upset my nurse."

"Yeah, sorry about that, hard to resist a good joke. I'll apologize on the way out," he replied.

The next group of patients were men and women, black and white, mostly young. All had multiple STDs. As they were brought in as a group, I finally asked a young, intelligent black guy why they were present as a group. "It's the party, Doc. A Wesson Oil party."

"What do you mean, Wesson Oil?"

"We're all strangers. First name only. Lots of meds to help you relax and also make the sex intense."

"Like what?"

"Oh, nitrous oxide, barbiturates, grass, alcohol, cocaine—you name it, you can have it. So everyone loosens up and perks up, disrobes, and greases up with scented oil. Then you pick a partner and go at it. Then another and so on until you're spent."

"You had ten partners in one night?"

"Yeah, an especially good night."

"But only first names. You don't really know anyone?"

"That's part of the thrill, Doc . . . all new, no attachments, no responsibility, and best of all, no followup."

"So you don't know how to reach any of these women so we can treat them?"

"Honest, Doc. No clue."

The clinic proved popular. After several weeks the lead contact investigator, Carl, informed me we were seeing over seventy patients daily. The patients presented with all types of sexually transmitted diseases, including syphilis in all three clinical stages, as well as the nodule of granuloma inguinal, the huge swollen inguinal lymph nodes of lymphogranuloma venereum; also gonorrhea, even the new clinical form with blood stream spread to tendons and joints, and rampant chlamydia. Clinical specimens were carefully obtained and transported on Marta at the end of the day to the research laboratories at CDC.

Early one morning, Carl mentioned that the newspaper, *The Atlanta Journal-Constitution,* and the local TV station wished to have an on-site interview, and wanted to know if lunchtime was OK. Carl thought any outlet that publicized the new clinic meant reaching new patients quicker, resulting, therefore in earlier treatment, and perhaps reversing the local epidemic. Carl was employed by Fulton County, not the CDC or the Federal government. He had the tough job of attempting to trace disease contacts within the incubation period and give treatment before further spread.

My interview appeared briefly on TV but in full in the *Atlantic Journal-Constitution*. The information about the dual purpose of the clinic in patient care and research was straightforward. No politician was I.

Sid paced back and forth in front of my desk, hands flailing, face flushed, and voice louder than necessary.

"What were you thinking, Jack? You can't give an interview in a national newspaper and TV for God's sake without clearing it with me, and the Director too! Do you know where I've been the past hour?" he thundered.

"Here, shouting at me?" I countered.

"Not funny! I've been with the director. He is very upset. This project was all off the books, loaning you out to the Fulton County Health Department, seeing actual patients, and transporting live specimens on Marta! Good grief, the County Health Commissioner called this morning and tore into me." Paul collapsed into my chair, breathing heavily.

I let a minute of silence pass then asked, "What did you think of the actual interview, Sid?"

"Fine, fine. Actually really good. Once he calmed down, the director liked it, too. But no more interviews, Jack! Why don't you take tomorrow off, go make rounds with Dr. J. Willis Hurst, the most famous cardiologist in America, play squash, whatever, then show up Friday, low key, quiet. By the way, I've approved the part-time dermatologist to help you out on Fridays."

Sid sighed, looked out my window at the fine Spring campus, thought for a bit, and then asked, "Are you learning a lot down there?"

"Yes, daily. I'm seeing every conceivable STD. But the patients, Sid, the patients are out of control. They are having unsafe, frequent sex, often anonymously, and then later with their partners, almost always without protection. The investigations can't keep up. This is a perfect situation for an unmanageable epidemic. What if one of these bacteria becomes totally resistant to antibiotics or becomes more aggressive or a new disease entirely and unpredictably enters the chain of transmission? Things could go wild quickly!"

"Yes, all terrible possibilities. You do have a vivid imagination. Try to stay focused on the clinic, the mission we outlined; we're not into moral judgments or criticizing sexual practices." Paul slapped his legs, smiled warily, and marched on to his next meeting.

Cardiology rounds at Grady Hospital were a sacred ritual, attended by medical students, pharmacists, nurses, interns, residents, cardiology fellows, and the famous Dr. Hurst.

Dr. Hurst had written the standard textbook on cardiology and carried within him an encyclopedic knowledge of heart disease. After the case admitted to Grady Hospital the previous night was presented, Dr. Hurst turned to a thirty-year-old physician in a white coat and grilled him publicly, without mercy, about the details of congenital heart disease in adults. The sweat on the brow of the young physician's face could have watered a garden. Finally, the young physician faltered on one detail, and Dr. Hurst pounced and laughed and filled in the subtle answer. I turned to the fatigued intern beside me and whispered, "Boy I'm glad I'm not that med student. Brutal."

The intern hesitated then whispered back, "That's not a medical student, that's the Chief Resident in Cardiology." I filed away a memory note to stay in the back of the pack on subsequent rounds. The Chief Resident briefly introduced me to Dr. Hurst as a visitor from the CDC; Dr. Hurst met my gaze, shook my hand, and moved quickly on.

The following week was full of patients of every variety. I learned to discriminate the rotary spiral motion of treponema palladium (the pathogenic bacteria that causes syphilis) from the looping motion of nonpathogenic saprophytic treponema on fluid dark field examinations. I percutaneously aspirated the large inguinal buboes from LGV patients, relieving local pressure and speeding recovery. We discovered that we could grow the bacillus

(Klebsiella granulomatous) responsible for the disease granulomas inguinal in the patient's own plasma, but not on artificial media. Finally, Dr. Lane took the new specimens from the clinic from a patient's primary syphilis chancre (painless ulcer) and grew the fastidious T. palladium in the testis of rabbits. From these organisms he developed a new and better diagnostic serologic test, the FTA-ABS.

Near the end of a Thursday clinic, Jenny brought back a young black woman, Serena, with severe abdominal pain. Serena had previously been treated for pelvic inflammatory disease (PID), and she felt her current pain meant a reoccurrence. The pain, however, was more pronounced in the lower right quadrant of the abdomen, raising concern for appendicitis. I suggested she go to Grady Hospital Emergency Room.

Jenny frowned and said, "Are you sure this isn't PID, Doctor A.?"

"No, I'm not sure, Jenny. But if it's appendicitis and if we send her home with a wish and a prescription, the appendix could rupture and cause life-threatening peritonitis. She needs to see a surgeon."

Jenny's foot began to tap the floor, and her frown deepened. "This is not so simple. The patient doesn't have a car and neither do I. And the Grady ER is a total zoo! And black people form a long, separate line at the zoo. Could be a five-hour wait," she explained.

"I'll go with you, and Carl will drive us to the ER. We'll stay until she is taken care of," I replied.

So we all drove to the Grady Hospital ER, Carl dropping us off among a sea of ambulances, the sick and injured standing, sitting, and lying on gurneys stretching as far as the eye could see. The ER nurse waved us to a stretcher, took Serena's vital signs, and informed us of a probable five-hour wait before a doctor was available. At that point, I informed the nurse that I was a doctor and needed to talk to the ER Intern. Jenny's frown returned, anticipating conflict. Ten minutes later, the intern, a young man my age and height, dressed in a short white coat and white starched pants, rounded the corner, and looked us up and down.

"What's the problem? The nurse says you're a physician. True?" he asked.

"Yes, I am, and I think our patient has appendicitis."

"Where did you come from?" he replied.

"She presented at the downtown new STD clinic thinking she had PID," I said.

"The VD clinic, huh. And you're the new VD doc, the one on TV." His voice was now condescending. He looked away, then down the long corridor of waiting souls.

"True, but I am also on the faculty of Emory Medical School," I countered.

"Uh huh, you look about my age. How could you be on the faculty of my medical school?" he questioned.

I reached into my back pocket and procured my new Emory faculty card. The intern took the card and looked again at us, two black women and a white man, now a little less sure of himself.

"You know, Doctor, last week I made early-morning rounds at Grady Hospital with Doctor J. Willis Hurst. Very impressive man. He shook my hand, welcomed me to the faculty, and asked me to call him if I encountered any problems. Do you think I need to call him?" I asked.

"Dr. Hurst? OK, no, you don't need to call him. Nooooo sir. Where is your patient?" he questioned.

We walked over to Serena, who was lying quietly on the gurney. The intern pulled the privacy curtain back and began to examine her. Thirty minutes later, the surgeon appeared, nodded politely to Jenny and me, repeated the physical exam, and told the nurse to draw blood and prepare Serena for the operating room. In the OR, the swollen appendix was removed, and Serena made a rapid recovery.

Clinic popularity grew, and fortunately Dr. Sid had allowed us to hire a part-time physician for Fridays. Nelson was our new physician, a private-practice dermatologist in his mid-thirties. Nelson was tanned, relaxed, good natured, and confident. His hair was styled, his Brooks Brothers sport coat fitted, his fingernails trimmed, and his blue tie neatly centered in the collar of his lightly starched shirt.

"How are we so fortunate, Nelson, to have a board-certified Emory graduate dermatologist at our humble clinic?" I asked.

Nelson smiled broadly, his teeth white and perfectly aligned.

"Atlanta is a great city, Jack. Wonderful climate, great restaurants, and lots to do. All sorts of cultural and athletic activities. I set out my shingle in Marietta, a fine suburb just north of Atlanta. Unfortunately, there is no shortage of dermatologists, or for that matter any physicians in Marietta. But I'm optimistic. So I need a little cash flow to keep the ship afloat. This work looks simple enough," Nelson enthused.

Nelson was a good diagnostician, but easily frustrated by patients who failed to follow his precise instructions or relapsed and returned. Billie-Jo was just such a patient. Billie-Jo was a single truck driver in his mid-forties, highly sexually active, and a frequent return visitor for a variety of STDs, but usually gonorrhea. He was also huge, well muscled, often unbathed, very opinionated, and noncompliant with condom use. The investigators tried to follow up with his numerous sexual contacts, but the women were often out of state, spanning his several-thousand-mile interstate truck route. Billie-Jo now returned to the clinic with throat pain and a painful urethral discharge, both almost certainly due to gonorrhea. Nelson was disgusted by everything Billie-Jo represented. Nelson shot large-volume doses of penicillin into each of Billie-Jo's generous buttocks and in a spirit of invention and pique, offered him a secret cure, "so it won't come back, ever." Billie-Jo eagerly agreed to the new treatment.

Without my knowledge, Nelson slipped out to his BMW and retrieved a bottle of methylene blue, an antibacterial dye. Nelson painted Billie-Jo's tongue and penis blue, and sent him on his way, laughing to himself at his prank. What Dr. Nelson did not tell Billie-Jo was that the methylene blue did not wash off, a fact that became abundantly clear in the large men's common urinal bathroom at the Sunday Atlanta Falcon's football game. First one and then all four of Billie-Jo's truck driver friends spotted his generous blue penis, then his blue tongue, laughing and pointing until the whole men's room was in an uproar. Billie-Jo was subsequently nicknamed the Blue Tiger.

Monday at 8:00 a.m. sharp, right as the clinic opened, Billie-Jo was at the door looking for Dr. Nelson, threatening to teach him a lesson with his big fists. We were able to calm Billie-Jo down by removing most but not all of his blue tint, reassuring him it would eventually wear off his tongue by daily scrubbing with a tooth brush. He vowed to return.

Dr. Nelson showed up on Friday looking like a different man. There were dark circles around his eyes, he hadn't shaved for several days, and his face exhibited an uncharacteristic twitch. He was unable to sit still for more than a few moments.

"Nelson, good grief man, what's happened to you?" I asked.

"You're not going to believe this, Jack. Saturday night my wife took our daughter and her two little friends to a movie, so I went downtown to see a Flames hockey game on my own. After the game, I was walking toward Peach Tree through a side alley. Two men ran in front of me; the second man caught the first, threw him on a parked car and stabbed him twice with a knife. The attacker looked left then right, but never saw me watching in the alley, then dropped the first man to the ground and ran off. I ran quickly to the man gasping on the ground, who was already dying, and did CPR. He died a minute later. I called the police and rescue squad and identified the murderer in a line-up. Apparently the murder was drug-payoff-related. The police warned me I was the only witness and to quote the police, 'These are really bad guys.' I can't sleep and I'm worried they will find out who I am and come after me and maybe my family!" Nelson's hand trembled as he fidgeted with his pen.

I then had to tell Nelson about Billie-Jo and his outraged threat. Nelson decided to skip the Friday clinic, shook my hand, and told me he would not be back. Nelson had passed over a line that separates the safe and predictable life of upper-class Americans to the random, violent, startlingly anxious life of urban Americans.

Jenny greeted me the following Friday at the clinic door. "He's gone, Doctor Armstrong. Dr. Nelson has left Atlanta. He apparently gave a written deposition about the murder, packed his family up, and fled. He's under some sort of witness protection."

The clinic continued to grow, and Fulton County decided to hire a full-time doctor to replace the borrowed CDC doctor. I stepped back over the line to the safety of research and reflection. The clinic staff had a goodbye lunch, and the nurses presented me with a handmade beer mug, decorated with one man dancing in a line with six women. We were all smiling.

Leaving the downtown Atlanta STD Clinic, I returned to the CDC and being home on time. Dave, Jean's father, sat in our biggest chair in the living room, fine, straight bourbon on the rocks on the side table, and baby Andy, just two months old, cradled in his arms. Dave had been a hard sell on our marriage, as he was an Ohio college football player and friend of Ohio State Coach Woody Hayes. Dave held a dim view of Michigan, Ohio State's chief rival, all things liberal or new at all for that matter, and scoffed at modern fashion and music. Nevertheless, even a conservative real estate agent could not conceal his joy at being invited to hold the first grandchild, and later that night to attend perhaps the baseball game of the decade.

"Doo da doo, what's with you?" Dave murmured as he rocked our blond-haired baby. "What's going to happen tonight? Are we really going downtown to watch baseball history?"

"Yes, Dave. Great seats. A sellout. Hank Aaron's going to hit number 715 tonight—I can feel it."

"How's the city taking it? There's been a lot of racial tension here, Jack." Dave swirled his bourbon and took a deep, appreciative sip.

"Now that's the question. He's received death threats and taunts, but at the same time he's clearly the team leader."

Hank Aaron was a remarkable man. He could play all aspects of the game with considerable skill. He was a great power hitter, smacking over thirty home runs in a season fifteen times, and had a lifetime batting average of .305. He could also field, steal bases, and throw a runner out at second from deep right field. Aaron was lean, focused, and family- and community-oriented. He had experienced overt racism in his career, often being required to use separate lodgings from the white players in the sixties. Yet he was not a bitter or angry man and was popular with his teammates.

"Bobbie, my co-teacher, says they shouldn't count the record even if he hits number 715. He says with more games and new bats Babe Ruth should keep the record," Jean said, her even tone suggesting exactly what she thought of her co-teacher's suggestion.

Dave laughed, "Actually the Babe played 150 games in 1927 and Aaron will be lucky to play 110. The bat length, diameter, type of wood and weight are regulated."

Susan, Jean's sister, just couldn't hold back any longer. "But Bobbie is a self-proclaimed red neck racist. In my school, almost everyone is cheering for Hank."

Jean nodded; her school was rooting for Aaron as well.

"Well, fans, we'll be there to see firsthand tonight!" I answered.

We had good seats behind first base. Esther, Jean's Mom, was not a sports fan, but was thrilled by the occasion. Dave was in his element and bought us all popcorn and hot dogs. The stadium was packed with 53,775 enthusiastic fans, the largest crowd to attend a game at the Atlanta stadium. In the fourth inning, April 8, 1974, Hammering Hank Aaron hit a home run into deep left field, number 715, breaking the great Babe's record. The people went crazy, several breaking through the barrier to run the bases with Aaron. The crowd, white and black, cheered without reservation. He was our hero. When Dave and Esther left Sunday night, Dave clasped my hand, kissed Jean and Andy, and thanked me for the best weekend ever.

JACKSON HOLE

Jackson Prison was the maximum security prison for a violent state during violent times. As an internal medicine resident at the University of Michigan in Ann Arbor in 1976, I was on my way to Jackson Prison to staff a prisoner day clinic for five days. The way from cerebral Ann Arbor through rural Jackson farmland to the prison passed through three separate worlds connected by road, but not by experience.

Jackson prison was huge, dark, and foreboding. Two armed guards greeted and escorted me through a series of locked gates. No idle talk escaped their set and serious lips. The prison corridors stretched out like rural Jackson byways. Our steps echoed as we walked toward the prison interior. All windows were barred; the cement floors were scrubbed and polished, matching the solid grey walls. We stopped at a metal office door guarded by two additional, somber, rifle-toting guards.

The first guard barked, "We gotta register you, Doc."

"Whose office is this?" I asked, facing a solid metal door.

"The warden's," he replied.

"Does he come to the clinic?" I asked.

"He's a she, and no, she doesn't go to the clinic. She comes in the morning, leaves in the evening. Don't see her much. Safer behind them barred windows," he pointed to a single shaded, barred window.

The guard disappeared into the office. I looked around for the clinic. Although the setting shouted danger, I was reassured by the large guards with guns.

Okay, I reasoned quietly, *there are some serious bad guys here but it looks like they've planned for that,* logic that was befitting of Ann Arbor, but not Jackson Prison.

The guards emerged from the warden's vault. I briefly saw the warden's face appear and disappear in the tinted window, but she was too busy to come out to talk. We resumed another long corridor march which eventually deposited us in a large room overlooking the prison yard. Ten men in white, starched uniforms were talking together. As we approached, the talking ceased.

"Okay, Doc, here you are. This is your home," the first armed guard laughed.

"You're not staying?" I asked.

"Nah, these trustee nurses will give you all the help you need. I'll be back at 4," he stated, looking first at me, then the collected trustees, then the open door.

The trustees laughed. A couple guys exchanged shoulder slaps.

Louis, the lead trustee and the largest human being alive outside of superhero movies, emerged from the pack and walked over to greet me.

"Hey, Doc, it's just you and us, huh? Gimme five!" he thundered.

Louis looked like he lived in the weight room. His biceps were as big as my head. His neck was shaped like an oak tree trunk. His long black hair was slicked back with Vaseline, not shaved short like the regular inmates. His alert, white face was broad, scarred, and filled with expression—smile and scowl crossing over in an instant. He smelled of Ivory soap, the prison brand. His huge hand guided me over to the treatment desk to meet the other trustees. I felt as if I had just entered a New York Giants huddle. Each guy slapped my shoulder and offered a high-five or a big palm.

"What is a trustee, Louis?" I asked.

"These guys have all been in Jackson a long time. They behave themselves, they get out of the cell to work the clinic as a trustee. A little freedom, a walk in the yard with your friends, and some privileges—it's an honor, man!" he explained.

"So we do this together, each day, right?" I asked.

"Yeah, Doc. We worked real well with Dr. Steward last week. Kind of a nervous guy, but he brought us a nice box of cigars the second day, and we did just fine after that. Generous man," Louis elaborated.

I thought for a minute, maybe less. "What's your favorite cigar, Louis?" I asked.

"Cubans, thanks!" he replied.

The clinics were busy, the exam rooms packed. I sat on a steel straight-backed chair behind a simple steel desk, both secured to the cement floor. Each trustee had a specific job assignment, such as taking vital signs, filling out a symptom card, completing an order, dressing a wound, or giving an injection. We broke briefly at 10 a.m. for coffee, one half hour for lunch in the clinic, and at 2 p.m. for a short walk in the yard. With familiarity, tongues loosened and stories flowed to a new and sympathetic listener. Many violent acts were complex events with mitigating circumstances, and most judgments and incarcerations were unfair, unjust, and soon to end. Remorse was in hiding.

On day three, Louis escorted me to the inpatient ward, what he called "Revenge Alley." When we arrived, he handed me off to the ward staff physician, Alice, a young, attractive brunette in tight pants and a loose surgical blouse, a recent University of Michigan graduate. As we made rounds, it became apparent that most of the patients were young to middle-aged men with paraplegia.

"What gives, Alice? Why all the paraplegics?" I asked.

"These guys were all in the drug trade. Distributers, you might say, who missed a payment. Do you remember pithing frogs with a needle in biology before you dissected them? Well, they were pithed with an ice pick, an alternative to death for the lucky."

Alice's gaze was direct, and she was a close talker, allowing me to take in her alluring scent.

"Alice, you must be careful here. These are all dangerous men who haven't seen a woman in many years. And you're very attractive. You'll drive them crazy," I lectured.

Alice laughed. "Yea, isn't this great? Not like being a priggish resident with all those dour professors and exhausted students. These men are edgy, dangerous, and so exciting. What about you, Doctor Jack? Which are you?" she asked.

Alice rested her hand on my arm just as one of the ward trustee nurses approached, a six-foot-two-inch, forty-year-old black man with huge biceps and many tattoos. His gazed at me with hostility, but when he shifted to Alice, he smiled slightly. Alice's hand lifted off my arm to his.

"Who's the guy, Alice?" he asked.

"He's the visiting university doctor, Marcus. He's on the ward just for the day. Don't worry about him, he's Chief Resident, even more righteous than the others." They both laughed at her joke. Marcus relaxed.

"Tell the Doc to leave his orders. We'll do what he asks," he said as he moved away.

"Alice, are you crazy? You can't be with this man. Louis told me this trustee is a convicted murderer with a bad temper."

"Oh, calm down, Jack. We all make mistakes in a passion; that doesn't mean we're bad people or need to pay for our decisions forever. Times are a changin', you know," she replied before humming the popular Bob Dylan tune she had just referenced.

"Yes, the times are a changin', Alice, but not this guy. Be careful, for God's sake," I warned.

We finished rounds late, as the lot of prison paraplegics was fraught with many humiliating complications, including festering pressure ulcers, fecal impactions, in-and-out bladder catheterizations, and endless tedium. Alice was gentle and thorough, a good doctor when focused on the task at hand. Alice would later orchestrate a notorious prison breakout attempt to free her murderer lover and his friend, involving a dramatic, commandeered helicopter escape. She lost her life at the car rendezvous.

On day four, the clinic routine trudged by uneventfully. Louis ran a tight ship. At 3 p.m., Louis escorted prisoner 1177 to the opposing steel chair, slapped his clinic card on the desk, and instructed the patient, Malcolm, to keep it brief. Louis ambled to the clinic entrance door to survey the waiting crowd. Malcolm's thin, tight face was dominated by large, penetrating brown eyes. His left eyelid twitched rhythmically.

"I got a bad headache, Doc," he stated.

"How long has your head hurt, Malcolm?" I asked.

"A long time, man. I need a shot!" he demanded.

"What is the cause of your headache?" I replied.

"I see a dumb Doc every week. Same headache, same talk, same shot," he retorted.

"Let me check you over, Malcolm," I stated.

Malcolm's thin, muscular arms were scarred with needle tracks. Although his left eyelid twitched constantly, his neurological exam was unremarkable. His skin was thickened with keloid scars, probably from old knife wounds. Many of his teeth were missing, as was a portion of his tongue, bitten during a drug withdrawal seizure.

"Malcolm, your headache should not go on this long without our knowing why. I'm going to arrange a brain CAT scan at the university," I explained. University tests were rarely ordered by the moonlighting residents. Diagnosis relied on a physical exam and the patient's history. Treatment was usually empiric. Much extra paperwork awaited any ambitious Resident.

"I do not want a damn CAT scan, Doc. Give me the shot!" Malcolm exploded.

I looked down at the sparse clinic record. Each week for six months Malcolm had appeared in the clinic with a headache and received an injection of 100 mg of intramuscular Demerol.

"We need to know why you're having these headaches, Malcolm," I replied.

Malcolm leaned forward in his chair until his warm breath was in my face. "Give me the fucking Demerol shot, Doc, or I'll kill your ass," he hissed.

My tongue seemed glued to my palate, my pulse increased, and verbal expression failed me.

A dark shadow appeared in front of my eyes and disorientation overtook me. Was I passing out? My vision slowly cleared and a big face with a wide, toothy smile was looking directly at me. The face said "It's alright, Doc, I'll take care of this."

Louis's steely neck pivoted to Malcolm, perhaps an inch separating them.

"Malcolm, do you know about Jackson Hole?" he asked.

"Yeah, Louis, it's the pit—solitary, dark as hell itself, and too tight to stand in," Malcolm replied.

"And do you know, Malcolm, who can put you in that hole for 48 hours, right now, no questions asked? Only the warden and this doc," Louis stated.

Louis's head rose like a bobber to look down at us. Malcolm's eye twitched double-time.

"When is your last day here, Doc?" Malcolm asked.

"Friday," I replied.

Malcolm rose slowly from his steel chair and turned to Louis. "No Jackson Hole, Louis," he demanded.

Louis nodded at the clinic door and Malcolm exited quickly.

Louis sat down in the steel patient chair, overflowing onto the table.

"Cuban cigar, Doc?" he asked, pulling out two of the fine cigars I purchased Tuesday.

FA'A SAMOA

The sleek jet plane began its gradual descent, aiming toward the lighted peninsular landing strip, a jeweled avenue leading from air to land, from one civilization to another. We glided to a stop at a traditional wooden airport, the entrance to tropical Tutulia, the largest and most populated island of American Samoa. Even in the evening dark we could see the mountainous outline surrounding the airport, not bare like the Rocky Mountains, but verdant and dense.

The cabin stirred as the two-thousand-mile flight from Hawaii concluded. Andy, our blond-haired two-year-old, was asleep on my lap. From the window, the Pacific Ocean sparkled in the moonlight, and my wife Jean stretched and yawned. Only twenty-six years old, with long dark hair, she gazed out at the stunning approach. We were the guests of Project Concern, a relief organization that matched physicians willing to work abroad as unpaid volunteers with developing countries desperate for supplemental medical hands. Pago Pago was the capital of American Samoa, a multi-island set of volcanic jewels glistening in the Pacific Ocean, five thousand miles from California.

Since selling our car for airfare and renting our home for six months, I had been immersed in the study of the Polynesian language and tropical diseases. English was a spoken second language only in the capital, Polynesian the first language of the Tutulia countryside and the remote out islands. Jean had read Margaret Mead's famous book, *Coming of Age in Samoa*, which graphically depicted Samoa as the last, best refuge of true Polynesian culture. We had agreed to immerse ourselves in the culture, language, food, and people as much as possible, not to stand apart as expatriates. From Mead's description of the complexity of Samoan society we recognized the many barriers to outsiders. We also knew from Somerset Maugham's short story, "Rain," how the tropical climate could grab you emotionally. Jean planned to be active teaching English as a second language to the children of Korean fishermen.

Disembarking, the air was warm and humid, the monsoon season soon concluding. The fragrance of tropical flowers mixed with the damp aroma of wet vegetation. The greeters were all Polynesian, dressed in colorful lava-lavas, with long shirts. Our host, Dr. Rob, was nowhere to be seen. We hailed a cab to the only island hotel, The Rainmaker, spread out on a peninsula facing deep Pago Pago Bay and the dramatic Rainmaker Mountain. Rain figured in Mead's and Maugham's descriptions of Samoa, as over two hundred inches fell during the monsoon season. We hoped to avoid the so-called tropical gloom that accompanied the monsoons by arriving just at its end. The US we left behind in 1976 was also emerging from the gloom of the Vietnam War. After four years of medical school, two years of epidemiology at CDC, and an additional two years of intense training as an internal medicine resident, I was ready for a less-structured life before starting a research fellowship in infectious diseases. Wonder and expectation filled us, rather than gloom.

LION IN THE NIGHT

The next day, after a breakfast of papaya, fresh bread, and coffee, Dr. Rob picked us up to drive to the Lyndon Baine Johnson (LBJ) Tropical Medical Center. Rob, a pulmonologist (lung specialist) in his mid-fifties who, ironically, was a chain smoker, was also an escapee from litigious California. His shy and unhappy wife and exuberant twelve-year-old son accompanied him. All the physicians lived closely in a small expatriate community contiguous to the hospital to permit quick access for night call and emergencies. Five physicians and seventeen Samoan and Fijian medics provided good care to over thirty-five thousand people. Our simple quarters were newly constructed, made storm resistant after the last typhoon swept away the previous, less-resilient structures. The cement foundation supported sturdy cement walls. The roof was also solid and typhoon-secure to fit the island motif. The low, one-story hospital building was visible across a verdant courtyard. The lush jungle and steep mountains framed the courtyard. Our home interior was sparse, but comfortable.

Two weeks after our arrival, Israel, a sixty-five-year-old retired Philadelphia internist, and his warm and gregarious wife, Fran, arrived to occupy adjacent quarters. Israel and Fran quickly became friends as well as Andy's surrogate grandparents.

Dr. Rob walked me through the medical center with a few private rooms and several wards. I met the Samoan surgeon and the pediatrician, Peter, both young, friendly, "glad to have you" guys. Our sole obstetrician was Australian, good-natured, and low-key. The rest of us were grateful not to be delivering babies at midnight. Israel worked in the ER with a core of skilled medics. Rob and I, along with several medics, ran the inpatient service and outpatient clinics. We had a functioning but small laboratory with good microscopes. Radiology was a single fluoroscope machine that we ran ourselves. The LBJ Tropical Medical Center was the prime referral facility for all the Samoan Islands, the only hospital with a real operating room and reliable diagnostic capabilities. The hospital was single level, the patient rooms spacious and often open to the air from large windows. Almost always families slept on mats beside patient beds and performed many basic care functions such as bathing and assisting with meals. Finding families for a patient conference was never an issue.

Our spacious but sparse apartment took on the feeling of a home with woven floor mats and colorful wall decorations. We rose with the sun, as daybreak was full of the sounds of the jungle and farm animals: roosters calling, birds singing, pigs grunting. Andy was a sound sleeper, tired from hours walking the beaches and learning to swim in the Rainmaker pool. He padded to breakfast, his long, blond hair disheveled, hugging his favorite stuffed animals, Mister Hoot, a brown owl, and Dynamite Dix, a droopy dog. Sandy, our adopted German shepherd, joined us for breakfast outside our screen door.

After the long trip, I suited up for a jog with Sandy, who came with our expatriate compound. We jogged to the edge of the compound, then Sandy stopped abruptly, barking loudly, directly at me. No coaxing made Sandy move forward, so I jogged on alone down the winding road. About one-quarter mile into the run, I spotted a pack of thin, wild dogs at the road's edge, just as they spotted me. They turned their hungry, lean, and snarling faces toward me as I pivoted to spring back to the compound. As a former track quarter-mile runner, my pace quickened, but the dogs were faster and closed the space between us. As I approached the compound's edge, Sandy awaited me, standing alert, teeth barred. He growled and barked at the mangy pack, as if to say, "Just cross this line and you'll see what a big, well-fed German shepherd can do to you pitiful mutts." The pack broke up, barked, hesitated, then— whining and growling—backed down the road. Sandy trotted to my side, head high, mission accomplished. I had just received my first important lesson in following local expert advice.

All jobs, even in paradise, assume a certain reassuring routine. Early morning rounds in the hospital were followed by x-ray and EKG review, then morning and afternoon clinics. Families were omnipresent at the hospital bedside or clinic waiting rooms. My skill with the Polynesian language was passable, but greatly assisted by the bilingual nurses and eventually by a Hawaiian medical student.

Certain subjects were taboo between Samoan women and foreign male physicians, irrespective of language proficiency. The nurses quickly picked up on colloquial evasions in animated, long dialogues, which often ended with a succinct, extracted chief complaint, "She hurts when she pees." STDs were rare in men or women in Samoa.

After a brief break-in period, I was trusted for night call for 100 inpatients from 6 p.m. to 8 a.m. After dinner, on my first call night, the phone rang. The ward nurse was worried about a new patient, a village high chief (a "matai") admitted during the day from the ER. The nurse related his high fever, rapid pulse, and generalized pain. She requested I come back to the hospital to examine the matai. I hustled across the moon-lit courtyard into the hospital entrance and down the faintly lit ward hall to the patient's room. The chief was the lone patient occupying the room, a nod to his authority and importance. He was a large man in his late forties, handsome, muscular, restless in bed, sweat dripping from his forehead. His apprehensive family surrounded him, his groans feeding their anxiety. The young nurse took me aside to confide that he was not so sick upon admission, but that his temperature had since risen to 102 degrees, his pulse to 110, his muscles and joints ached, and his abdomen was hurting.

I introduced myself, reviewed his vague complaints, then began to examine the chief. As I worked my way down from examining his heart and lungs, I noticed a fine collection of herbs in his umbilicus. I looked up at the nurse who explained that the chief had first consulted the village medicine doctor who applied the herbs to the perceived pain source. When the herbs and chants did not relieve his pain, his family brought him to the ER. The admitting diagnosis was fever and abdominal pain.

I palpated his muscular but soft abdomen, probably not the fever source. As I worked my way down to his right knee, he guarded the knee from movement. The knee was markedly distended with fluid. As I moved the knee, he groaned, as did the now-closely-packed family. I asked the nurse for an aspiration syringe. After cleaning the knee, I attached the imposing needle to a large syringe to withdraw the fluid. All eyes, including the chief's, focused on the needle. A quick, animated conversation between the Chief and the nurse ensued.

She turned to me and said, "He trusts you. Do what you have to do. We have not done this before. Have you?"

I nodded yes, anesthetized the skin, and slowly inserted the needle into the bulbous knee, withdrawing fifty cc's of turbid, angry fluid. A low murmur of assent emanated from the family. I took the fluid to the laboratory, focused the microscope on the white-blood-cell-filled slides, searching for bacteria. But under the warming light, instead I found the needle shaped crystals of uric acid, signaling a diagnosis of gout. I returned to the bedside and the now-quiet crowd. I injected the colchicine (a medication specifically for treatment of gout) into his intravenous line. On the advice of the nurse, we both waited at the bedside for several hours. The temperature declined, and with its descent, the pain abated. The nurse smiled and nodded, and we reassured the family. The chief at last fell asleep, and I walked home under the full moon, slid into bed next to my warm and beautiful wife, who murmured, "Asleep now," and rolled over until dawn arrived two hours later.

After work duty, the expatriate physicians head to the sea to snorkel, swim, drink rum, and watch the spectacular sunsets. Andrew, the only attorney in Samoa, swam up to me at the reef's edge.

"Amazing, isn't it?" Andrew exclaimed. "Just over this reef it's 1,000 feet deep. Every creature in the dark sea lives there. But here, at six feet, there is just the coral, warm water, octopi, and tropical, colorful fish. But something even more exotic is about to happen, Jack, if you have a little courage."

I remembered well the first time Andrew encouraged me to have "a little courage." Andrew owned a small Hobie Cat sailboat, an eighteen-foot Catamaran that we sailed in the calm, long, and open Pago Bay. One afternoon he suggested we venture out of the harbor to test the wide Pacific Ocean. At first the brisk breezes and heightened boat speed were exciting and a challenge. But then, in an instant, real wind kicked in, followed by six- to eight-foot swells. Tacking back to the harbor opening proved technically and physically difficult, but we eventually succeeded after a couple of silent hours. As we entered the harbor to quiet water, we were passed by a large tiger shark. It seemed to be about the same size as the Catamaran. The shark had probably been out in the Pacific, hoping for us to overturn. Landing at shore, Andrew seemed exhilarated by the whole experience.

"Wow, Jack! That was really close!" he said. Andrew had been an indoor, corporate attorney in Los Angeles. In Samoa, as the only expatriate attorney, he managed to be outdoors much of the day, occupied by sailing and tennis. Thin, muscular, and very energetic, Andrew was wired for adventure.

"So, Jack, as I was saying on the boat before the breeze stiffened, if you have a little bit of courage, there's a very unusual, once-in-a-lifetime experience coming up next week," he said as he took a long tug on his rum-and-coconut-cream daiquiri.

Carol and Jean both said at the same time, "This better be good and much safer, Andrew."

"Listen, listen. Once a year the Coral Larva Upulu worms migrate en masse from the coral. And they are bioluminescent! They glow in the dark! An eerie yellow-green! You'll never see this again, ever!"

"But Andrew," interjected Carol, the practical girl, "tell Jack and Jean at what time we have to dive to see these glory worms."

"Well, at night, at 10 p.m.," he replied.

"OK, Andrew, and what else comes into the shallows to feed at night?" Carol asked.

"Sharks, of course, but just the small, safe, reef sharks, mostly," Andrew murmured, now subdued by his memory of the huge tiger shark that had followed our Hobie Cat into the harbor.

Finally, Jean and Carol agreed to the night dive, accompanied by large, underwater lights. We drove to the isolated beach in our old Honda with the hole in the floor allowing you to see the road pass by. Carol and I dove to the right, Andrew and Jean to the left. The large underwater lights illuminated our way to the reef 100 feet offshore. The night was quiet except for the low breathing of our snorkles. We turned off the lights as we approached the reef.

The sea became pitch black. Slowly, green-yellow worm-like larvae emerged from the coral. Hundreds, then thousands of bright larvae wiggled free of the reef, illuminating the water. Otherworldly, we were suspended in a silent, dark void, as green, swimming, new life engulfed us, then swam expectantly between and past us. As we swam back to shore, lights and souls ablaze, I heard Jean scream, followed by Andrew. We looked over to them, swimming frantically, then running to the beach.

"It came right into my light circle," Jean exclaimed, green eyes flaming."

"Jean, you knew the sharks feed at night!" Andrew exclaimed, his hands trembling as he brushed his hair back.

"But oh! Those Upulu," Jean exclaimed. "Have you ever seen anything so beautiful, so exotic?"

We gathered our equipment, dried off, and headed home, tired, but thrilled to the core. At our tropical apartment, we found Andy asleep in Fran's lap. Israel was asleep in the chair next to her, Sandy also asleep at their feet. Grateful were we to find these wonderful people.

About 10 a.m. each day, after morning rounds were complete and clinic soon to start, the physicians gathered for a cup of coffee and doctor talk about patients, diagnoses, and the day. Ham, our crusty Boston pediatrician, described the upcoming weeklong medical trip to the out-island clinics. The Samoan out islands were smaller than Tutuila, less populated, mountainous, ruggedly beautiful, hardly touched by Western customs—perhaps as close to original Polynesian culture as existed. The islands were visited only quarterly by a physician. The trip began with a flight on a single-engine plane between Tutuila and Tau, the largest out-island. The Samoans resented Margaret Mead for portraying them as promiscuous simpletons in her book. The Samoans were proud of their complex Polynesian culture, but also now careful to point out their adopted Christian faith. Only recently had young Polynesian women learned that an uncovered breast was shameful.

Dr. Rob turned to Ham. "I can't go now. Family issues. What about you, Jack?"

"Can Jean and Andy come along?"

"Why not? It's not only beautiful, but pretty safe," offered Israel, my perpetual advocate. The other docs nodded, perhaps content to stay safely home.

When we showed up early at the Pago Pago Airport, we found our young pilot inspecting his plane. He asked me to sit up front next to him.

"You must be quite an experienced pilot to make this flight over the open Pacific Ocean in a one engine plane," I offered.

"No, not really, Doc. I was a social worker in LA until six months ago when I got divorced. I flew for fun in LA. The divorce was ugly and I just had to get away. Came out here with no plans but to escape. The fruit company needed an inter-island pilot, mainly going to Western Samoa. We've made this trip to Tau once before and it went OK except for the landing. You have to approach the island over a big mountain, then drop like a rock on the other side to hit the dirt airstrip, really just a field, then brake to a stop to keep from flying into the jungle at the end of the field. Wait until you see the airport!"

I looked back at Jean; she flipped me the bird and turned to look out the window.

The plane rose quickly and beautiful, green Tutuila faded behind us as the broad, blue Pacific spread out in front of us. After an hour a small island appeared, fronted by a large rocky mountain. The pilot leaned toward me.

"This is it, Doc. I've got to fly up over that mountain, then drop to the landing strip. In case I pass out, let me show you a few of the controls."

"Pass out? Why would you pass out?"

"Well, I'm forty-five for one thing, and during the divorce— Jesus, I could have killed that woman—I developed this heart flutter. The pills and being away from that bitch and the fine rum have all helped, but who knows when it could strike again?"

"Great, that's just great. A one-engine plane in the middle of the Pacific ocean ascending to clear a mountain and you want to show me how to lower the landing gear? I looked back at Andy and

Jean, who held Andy's favorite stuffed animal, Mr. Hoot, in front of her face, eyes crossed and tongue sticking out straight at me.

"Don't be so jumpy, Doc. It's simple, really. This switch puts the gear down and this other one here controls the speed. Here we go." The plane crested the mountain peak then fell rapidly to a dirt landing strip and braked, flaps out. The plane skidded through the dusty strip to grind to a halt in front of a large mango tree with a wooden sign posted six feet up reading: "Tau Airport." Two jeeps awaited us.

"Oh my God, I thought we were going to die," breathed Jean.

"You have no idea," I said.

"Mr. Hoot's OK," ventured Andy.

We deplaned and headed for the jeep, driven by two stocky Samoan male medics, and sped to the clinic, a low building surrounded by open fales. The fales had bamboo mats on the floors and rolled up on the sides for wind and rain protection.

Our Tau clinics were packed with families from infants to budding teenagers. The Samoans are a stoic people who minimize symptoms, but chatted amicably with my young, Polynesian nurse interpreter. Diabetes, parasites, and arthritis are common. The second day our surgeon performed circumcisions on preadolescent boys. Boys who did not cry out in pain were rewarded with a highly prized chicken. All twelve boys went through surgery with only local anesthesia, without a whimper—honor and a chicken carrying the day. Later that night, we were invited to a Fia Fia (a festival). As the music played and all began to dance, Andy, dressed in a lava lava, also began to dance. He was served a wooden cup of fresh coconut juice. As he twirled across the dance floor, he tripped and upended the cup in the lap of the unsuspecting chief, a matai, or high chief. The music and dancing stopped, and all eyes pivoted to the chief and the little, blond-haired urchin. After a moment's pause, the chief flexed and pointed to his knee, remembering the night we met in the Pago Pago Hospital. Then the chief filled the night with his huge laugh and swept up Andy to sit on his lap. The music and dancing resumed and continued until late. The Polynesian dancing and music is sensuous, but never vulgar or crude. The best young women dancers sway not only to the music, but to the sea, the night, and to the rhythm and beauty of life.

We rose with the roosters the next morning, planning to fly from Tau to Olasinga Island. The plane was delayed, and the chief suggested we catch a ride on a large fishing boat arriving soon off the coast. Tau, unlike Tutuila, does not have a deep harbor, so the boat was boarded by paddling out in two outrigger canoes. The beach was crowded with Samoans, but we were the only travelers transported 300 yards offshore. As we approached the large, two-story boat, it was apparent the only way on was up, climbing a fishing net thrown over the side of the boat. I had Andy clutching Mr. Hoot on my back, and Jean was loaded with the backpack of necessities on her back, all of us to ascend the net and land on the deck. Our seats for the sea voyage were two large banana crates.

The clinic in Olasinga was full and busy. The next day we planned to travel to the last out-island, Ofu—small, isolated, mountainous, and never visited by tourists. The jeep transported us through the tropical jungle to the ocean's edge; a 100-yard channel separated the two islands. Our driver reassured us an outrigger canoe taxi would soon appear to cross the channel. At high tide the channel was too deep to cross on foot, but at low tide, a rocky coral ledge permitted passage with the sea only waist high. The day passed, the tide flowed out, but no outrigger taxi appeared. Sunset was not far off. We decided spending the night at water's edge was risky, so once again I loaded Andy on my back, Jean hauled on the backpack, and we tied ourselves together to walk on the coral ridge. As we crested the Ofu beachhead, the outrigger taxi arrived, the friendly driver laughing at our journey, and mentioned the timelessness that envelopes all who live so close to nature. We loaded the canoe and paddled to the village. Most of the villagers turned out to greet us and tussle Andy's long blond hair. Protectively, Jean picked up Andy to hold him close as we walked to the seaside village.

The medical clinic was conducted in the home of our host nurse. Her home was situated on a rocky bluff overlooking the blue Pacific Ocean, the sheer rock Ofu Mountain rising straight up a half mile behind us. As we rested on the open veranda that night, the ocean rhythms rocked us to sleep, far from home, but yet at home.

Partway through the next day clinic our host nurse asked us our dinner preference, offering to send her ten-year-old son, Tupua, diving for fresh lobster. Tupua returned at sunset with lobsters, but also a pouch full of pearls. Unfortunately, he placed his last pearl finds in his ears, the pouch already fully packed. The pearls were now impacted in his auditory canal, and his ears were hurting from manipulation. Unable to dislodge the pearls with water or lubricant, I attached a thin surgical suture with superglue to the pearl, lubricated the canals, and gently pulled the prizes free. Like the circumcised boys, Tupua was steady, tearful, but quiet. We shared a dessert of papaya and mango, the evening and trip coming to an end.

After we returned to Tutulia, Andrew and Carol suggested a weekend trip to Apia, the capital of Western Samoa, an independent nation. We arranged a flight and reservations at Aggie Gray's Inn, a famous destination owned by an aging female legend who had helped lead the island resistance during World War II. The Western Samoan Islands are even more remote than American Samoa, without evidence of Western incursion and development. The scenery and beaches were beautiful, but poverty was widespread. Seriously ill patients were flown to Pago Pago to the LBJ Tropical Medical Center. Our time in Apia was fun, but too quick; and soon we were returned to the airport by a friendly cab driver, Reupena. We were so taken by Reupena's tales of Samoan culture that we left Andy's favorite friend, Mr. Hoot, in the back seat of the cab.

The return home to Tutulia was welcome, but Andy was disconsolate, asking at night, after his bedtime story, "Where is Mr Hoot? I want Mr. Hoot!" Jean made up a good cover story of Mr. Hoot's adventures in Apia, but we knew the stories would only have a short-term effect. Fortunately, Reupena had given me his business card in case we returned to Apia. In reply to my letter, he wrote back stating he had found Mr. Hoot in the cab, but the only safe passage back was by return flight. Fourteen long nights later we picked up Andy's special delivery package at the Pago Pago Airport. Andy and Jean tore into the package; Andy retrieved the little owl, hugged him to his chest and said, "Mr. Hoot had a long trip!"

As our time in Samoa was soon to end, night hospital call continued one last time. The last evening the night medical nurse called about a post-operative patient with a high fever following a transfusion. The patient was young, but very ill, with shaking chills and a rapid pulse. I hurried out into the night, but quickly became aware of the consuming aroma of tropical flowers and vegetation newly revitalized by rain. The ocean could be heard in the distance, lapping against the beach. I knew I would never forget this wonderland of nature.

As I arrived in the hospital, I remembered our laboratory director fretting that we did not screen our blood before transfusion for filaria, a common Samoan parasite that could lead to disfiguring enlargement of the legs and scrotum or Elephantiasis. Easy to treat early, the filaria were difficult to dislodge once entrenched in the lymphatics. Prompt diagnosis and treatment was crucial. The young patient was agitated and delirious with fever. We sent specimens for all the usual tests and suspended the transfusion. I took a fresh sample of his blood to examine microscopically in the lab with the hematology technician. And there it was, a thin filarial larval worm stretched out among the red blood cells. We started the patient on Diethylcarbamazine, and his temperature declined during the night. Three days later he walked out of the hospital.

On our last night in Pago Pago, our friends Fran and Israel threw a going away party. Many guests came by, including intrepid Andrew and Carol, Peter, the lead Samoan pediatrician, as well as several of the Samoan medics, chiefs, and Korean fisherman. We drank rum punch, danced to Samoan music, and the chiefs presented us a beautiful tapa bark parchment painted by hand with brown tree pigment. When our plane lifted off from Pago Pago Airport in the morning, we knew a portion of our hearts would always be joined to the island and its people.

THE FINAL SHOCK

I was sitting at a patient's bedside on the fifth-floor medical ward, listening to a man tell his story of how one moment he was well and the next a shiver struck him and his raging fever started, when I received the first page to the Emergency Room. "Dr. Armstrong. Code Blue, ER." Everyone knew Code Blue meant cardiac arrest. What wasn't as well known was the Red Button, which was mine for twenty-four hours, a rotating physician assignment for patients arriving in the ER without a private physician. I excused myself from the bedside and ran to the stairwell, then down the stairs to the ER. The nurses were rapidly hooking up the patient to the cardiac monitor. Oxygen was inserted in the patient's nose and an IV was already running. To my surprise, the patient on the stretcher was a young, fit man, handsome, and unscarred.

"Ventricular fibrillation, Dr. Armstrong," the ER RN, Gloria, announced.

"Charge up the defibrillator!" I ordered.

CPR was ongoing—both chest compressions and mouth-to-mouth resuscitation. The respiratory therapist arrived, setting up the tray for intubation. The first full EKG confirmed ventricular fibrillation, a lethal heart rhythm so fast and irregular the heart is unable to pump blood.

We applied the shock pads to the patient's chest and pressed the paddles firmly. "All clear!" Gloria shouted.

The first shock lifted the patient off the stretcher. All our gazes shifted to the monitor which remained in ventricular fibrillation.

We gave the patient IV Lidocaine, Bicarbonate, and Epinephrine. We shocked his chest repeatedly, but the ventricular fibrillation persisted. We intubated and ventilated him. Time raced by. The small circle of the resuscitation team was now joined by a larger group of onlookers. Fifty minutes is a long Code Blue, but the patient was so young, I felt we had to try every option.

"Time to call it, Doc?" asked Gloria softly.

"Do we have any Bretylium?" I asked. Bretylium was a new, exotic drug in the early eighties that was thought to possess the potential to make refractory ventricular fibrillation susceptible to electrical defibrillation. I had heard the drug discussed at a conference at the University of Michigan, but had never used it for an actual patient.

"We have one new vial. We're opening it now. Should we push it IV?" asked Gloria in a questioning tone.

"Yeah, Gloria, give it now!"

Gloria raised her eyebrows, as the drug had never been used in Winchester either. With just a few seconds' hesitation, Gloria infused the full vial. We waited the mandatory sixty seconds to allow the drug to circulate to the heart, eyes glued to the chaotic monitor.

"One final shock, Doc?" Gloria asked, both her eyebrows now in a serious arch of doubt.

We charged up the defibrillator and applied the paddles to the chest wall.

"Three hundred and sixty joules," I requested.

"Ready to go," whispered Gloria.

I pressed the triggers and the patient again jumped from the gurney.

"Jesus, holy Christ! Normal sinus rhythm!" shouted Gloria.

"Check his blood pressure?" I asked.

"My loving God, it's here! Ninety over seventy!" exclaimed a flushed Gloria.

Sweat was pressing through my shirt, but my hands were steady. The room smelled of anxiety and a little burned flesh.

"Let's go to the ICU now!" shouted Gloria.

We settled Ren into the ICU, a cocoon of monitors and care-givers. When Ren was at last stable, I left the ICU to meet Ren's wife who waited in the family room. Other families in the room moved away, the story of Ren's dramatic arrest and resuscitation already spreading. Ren's wife, Pat, was a young, fit woman who had been crying, but who was now composed. I reviewed what had occurred in the field, ER, and ICU. She related the facts of Ren's hectic life, including two jobs, two daily packs of cigarettes, eight morning cups of coffee, and two six-packs of beer each night.

"Not much of a father or a husband, you know." She frowned and looked down at her hands now folded quietly in her lap. "I'm not sure I could have gone on with our life the way it was. Ren was like being married to a ghost."

"Ren is going to need you at his bedside. Someone to live for."

She sighed and looked away, then focused directly on my eyes.

"What will he be like when he wakes up?"

"We won't know for awhile. He was out for fifty minutes A long time. But CPR was started immediately and well maintained. We'll know better in a few days."

"Will he be a vegetable, Doctor?"

"No, but he may be a little frontal lobeish."

"What does that mean?"

"Well, after the brain is exposed to a lack of oxygen, the pa-tient may be childlike, emotional, and have poor short-term mem-ory. This state may be temporary and with time it could resolve itself. Will you be here at this time each day?"

Pat hesitated, folded and unfolded her hands, then again looked me directly in the eyes. "He's been kind to the children when he's around. He has a good soul—he's just lost his way. Yes, I'll be here for Ren."

Ren stabilized in the ICU. Gradually he was weaned from life support. Groggy at first, Ren recognized Pat, wept, then hugged her. He was slow to speak and amnestic to his resuscitation and ICU time. By day five Ren transferred to a medical room. Pat sat at his bedside and wept again when their children visited.

Eight days into his hospitalization, I stopped by Ren's room in the evening. He looked younger than thirty-eight. The dark circles rimming his eyes were fading, his dark complexion had improved, He was thin and fit, with his long hair brushed back. He wanted to talk. "Doc, I know why this happened. I just whipped myself to do more, coffee and cigarettes to get moving, beer to slow down. I guess my heart just gave out."

Ren's stress test and heart catheterization showed no blockages.

"Are you ready to change, Ren?" I asked.

"Cigarettes are gone! No more, period! I do love coffee though, and how about one six pack of beer at night?"

"It's good you're giving up the cigarettes, Ren, but I vote no more than four cups of coffee, maybe two beers at night, and one job."

"OK. Man, Doc, that's going to be tough."

"You've been given a second life, Ren. You may not get a third."

Ren slammed his fist into his hand and replied, "I told Pat I'd do whatever you said. We got a deal, Doc!" Ren reached out his hand for a firm shake. I held his hand for just a moment then moved on to finish rounds.

As years passed, Ren was a man of his word. Pat was the love of his life and their children grew and left for a path of their own, loved and supported by both parents. Ren worked hard, never smoked again, and battled daily to keep his promise of four cups of coffee in the morning and two beers at night. Ren underwent cardiac bypass at sixty-five but breezed through. We shook hands again when we both turned seventy and I, but not Ren, retired.

CLARE

Stretched out quietly on the gurney, Clare appeared childlike. Her thin arms were draped over the spotless white sheets, her skin clear and pale. The cardiac monitor called out her every heartbeat, the ventilator hummed each breath, and the IV pump clicked with the infusion of her life-support fluids. All was seemingly under control. The emergency room miasma of sweat, disinfectants, and bodily fluids floated above and through us.

"Real sad, isn't it, Doc?" Deb questioned. "Good-looking woman, terrible disease," she stated with a slight head wag. Deb was a seasoned ER nurse: capable, sturdy, clear-eyed, and a little cynical. I coached her two athletic daughters in soccer, along with my own petite-but-speedy daughter, Liz.

"Here, dress up, Doc. Time to go to work." Deb handed me the requisite yellow isolation gown, blue gloves, and grey mask. The year was 1984, the terror of the times was AIDS, and my new patient a victim. AIDS—foreign and devastating—was exploding, its transmission and way of transforming the immune system yet to be worked out. I was the Red Button Call Doctor assigned for twenty-four hours to care for patients without a private physician.

"What's her name, Deb?" I asked.

"Just 'Clare' her roommate told us."

Fully garbed, I began to examine Clare. She was thin, with bruised needle tracks that scarred her arms. White patches of thrush adhered to her tongue and mouth. Crackles like sandpaper rattled through my stethoscope as I listened to her lungs over the ventilator's hum. Her heart raced. Although thin and acutely ill, she was muscular and strikingly attractive.

"Look familiar to you, Doc?" Deb asked.

"I've never seen her before, but yeah, there is something familiar about her," I responded.

"The ER Docs say she looks just like Jane Seymour."

"OK, yes, I can see the resemblance," I said, as I lifted her eyelids to check her pupillary response, noting both eyes were green, not different colors like Jane Seymour's.

The chest x-ray hung from the wall view box. Dense white lines crossed through the dark airspaces of the lung.

"PCP (Pneumocystis carnii pneumonia), Deb," I offered.

"The radiologists think so, too."

"Let's move her to the ICU. Get the IV Bactrim going. She's going to get worse before she gets better. Is the roommate still here?"

"I'll bring her back, Doc. No family."

We hung the Bactrim, a sulfa antibiotic to kill the parasite, Pneumocystis, that ravages the lungs of immune compromised AIDS and cancer patients. Deb tidied up Clare for her roommate's visit.

Crystal, the roommate, was young, attractive, and both exhausted and apprehensive. She avoided eye contact.

"I'm Dr. Armstrong, Crystal. I'll be taking care of Clare in the ICU. Are you her roommate?"

"Yes, for the past year," she whispered. "She's been real sick all week—coughing, short of breath, hot, not eating. She's sliding downhill so fast. She wouldn't go see her own doctor because they had a falling out. She went off all her meds several months ago. Last night was terrible. She was gasping for breath. Her sides were killing her. I finally called the rescue squad. I told them to bring her here. Everybody was very careful but real jumpy. I think she's burned her bridges in Fairfax."

"What happened in Fairfax?"

"We're escorts, you know," she offered. "Clare was infected with HIV several years ago. Sometimes when she was angry, which was often, she'd tell the guys they didn't need to wear a condom. You can imagine they liked that. I told her she was killing them, as did the Fairfax doctor. She'd just laugh and say, "It serves them fucking right. What do you expect from a whore?"

"Is that why she lost her Fairfax doctor?"

Crystal shifted from foot to foot and sighed deeply. "Yeah, he got really mad and threatened her, then just signed off."

"Any family I should talk to?"

"No, her father died when she was ten. She is estranged from her mother. I think the mother let the uncle abuse her as a child. She was fucking him, too. We all got a story, Doc." Crystal sighed, looked away then at me, and said, "Clare is so full of hate."

We slid Clare onto a clean gurney and rolled her off the elevator into the ICU. The ICU is a kingdom apart. Each patient is in a cocoon, a separate room—the nurse, respiratory therapist, phlebotomist, and a parade of physicians quietly hovering over the silent, entombed patient. No one approached the room without full protection, an aura of caution pervading every movement. Clare remained on the respirator for four days, time for the antibiotics and steroids to slowly kill the parasite, allowing the lungs to begin healing. Clare was transferred to a private room, permitting some privacy to the emerging soul. Morning rounds started at 7:00 a.m.

As I entered the room, Clare was being attended to by a middle-aged African-American nurse's aide. Clare had finished bathing, and the Aide, Betty, was combing Clare's long brown hair, humming a spiritual hymn as she worked—a tender, fearless soul with gentle hands. I introduced myself while Betty toweled down Clare's hair and neck and reassured Clare she'd be back. Betty winked at me. We'd shared many patients.

"So you're the unlucky ID Doc," Clare stuttered.

"Yes, I'm Dr. Armstrong and you've been very ill. Do you remember much?"

"Just a blur, really. A few shadowy faces, an occasional touch. But I do remember gasping for breath, a terrible feeling, as if each breath was my last. How long am I going to be here?" Clare now looked at me directly, her large, green eyes like emeralds in a soft pale sea.

"At least one week. But you've responded to treatment. Each day is a little better. I'll need to restart your HIV meds before you go home."

I examined Clare, ordered her treatments, reassured the staff that her pneumonia was not contagious, and moved on to the next patient room. Betty slid in behind me to finish her work. The attending nurse, Faith, walked with me to the next room and asked if it was all right if we consulted the chaplain. The chaplain was a kind, patient man, a good listener, a Quaker of the best kind—a helper, not a judge. "Sure," I said, "Peter might help."

Peter knocked on Clare's hospital room door and asked if he could come in. After a long pause Clare said, "OK."

The room was empty, save one greeting card. Clare was sitting upright in bed, the hospital blanket and sheets folded neatly over her legs and hips. She was turned away from the door, staring out the far window. Chaplain Taurus introduced himself.

"I'm the chaplain. May I come in to talk?"

Clare did not answer for a minute, then turned with a look of hostility. "Chaplain. That's like a preacher, isn't it? You're the hospital preacher, right?"

"Yes."

"Yeah, well, you guys are some of my best customers. Fuckers like the rest of them. And you guys are some of the biggest assholes, too."

"I know, ministers can hurt people. And some are hard to get along with."

"What do you want, Chaplain?"

"If you want to talk, I'm here to listen."

Clare looked at Chaplain Taurus for a moment then looked away for a few minutes.

"What is there to talk about? I've had a crummy life. My Dad died young. My mother was a slut who didn't care about anything but herself. She let my asshole uncle rape me repeatedly, starting at age eleven. I became an escort at seventeen, serving a world of greedy pricks, including doctors and ministers." Clare looked at Peter with anger and distain, but remained quiet for several minutes. Then she smiled slightly and asked, "Chaplain, do you have a puppy?"

"Yes, I have a dog who was a puppy."

"That's the only time I've ever been loved. Really loved."

"How do you mean?"

"I was twelve. I found the puppy in a gutter. He was scrawny and weak. I picked him up and he whimpered and started licking my hand. I took him home and showed him to my mother. She said she didn't have time to take care of a damn dog, and if I wanted to keep him, I would have to care for him myself. So I fed him some milk and a couple pieces of bread. Mom got mad at that. She said I was feeding him our food that was hard to get. So I stole some money and went with a friend to buy him some puppy food and a food and water dish. After that, we played with the puppy in a vacant lot. I would throw a stick, and the puppy would fetch it and bring it back to me. It was fun! He would jump up and lick my hands and face! I found a collar and a piece of rope and we would take walks around the neighborhood. We had so much fun!"

Clare looked again out the window and when she turned back, her face was softer and a few tears appeared.

"Puppy slept with me in my bed except when my uncle came in to fuck me. Then he would throw puppy out of my bed. One night he threw puppy down so hard he yelped and then lay still. After my uncle finished with me, I picked puppy up. He was still breathing, but was all bloody. He died in my arms. My friend and I buried him in a shoebox in the vacant lot where we had so much fun. I tried to say a prayer for him, but I don't know how to pray and neither did my friend."

Clare paused for a moment and her face was again hostile.

"My mother said she was glad my puppy was dead. She said that was one less thing for her to worry about. As if she ever worried about anything but herself. But I loved my puppy and he loved me." A tear rolled down Clare's cheek.

"Did you give your puppy a name?"

"I just called him Puppy. But I loved him so much and he was the only thing that ever loved me." More tears glistened in her beautiful green eyes.

"Clare, as you share this with me about your puppy and friend, I hear a caring, loving, and giving person who has been hurt so many times in her life."

Clare looked at Chaplain Taurus for a long moment, then covered her face and began to sob quietly. The sobbing intensified and her shoulders shook. After a few moments, Chaplain Taurus rested a hand lightly on Clare's shoulder. She reached up, took the Chaplain's hand, held it against her cheek, and continued to quietly sob.

"I'm all right now, chaplain."

"I'll call the nurse back in. Would you like me to look back in on you later?"

"Yes, please, chaplain."

By the sixth day, Clare was almost back to normal. Her lungs were clear. The dry, white mouth patches were replaced by normal pink mucosa, and the oxygen prongs were finally removed from her nose. Time to talk reality. Peter, the chaplain, had left the room after spending what seemed like half the day listening to Clare. Peter had long hair, a trimmed beard, and the kindest eyes in the Shenandoah Valley. Clare sat up at the side of the bed, now composed with a cheerful expression of bemusement.

"Serious talk time now, Doctor?" she murmured.

"Lots to cover, Clare. Medications, diet, activities, and follow-up appointments. All clear?"

She nodded.

"And then there is the issue of practicing your occupation with disclosures and protection."

"We seem to be in agreement on everything but the last subject, Doc."

"You have to be honest, Clare, and insist on protection."

"No and no, Doc. My clients are wealthy men and they don't like the condom of the common man. If I tell them I have HIV . . . end of my business."

"Clare, you're handing those men a death sentence for the price of one night's pleasure."

"Too fucking bad. Their choice, you know." The bemused look was replaced by one of anger and condescension. "Go ahead, Doc. Play the good boy. Call the Fairfax police. I'll even give you a name. Sergeant Frazier. You'll see, they don't care. Too much trouble, too much other stuff like murders. I'm just offering a good fuck for bucks."

"We have to resolve this, Clare. I can't fix you up to go out on the kill."

"Yeah, I'm the killer! What about my bastard uncle who raped me? And my weak mother who valued other men more than her daughter? And what about all these rich pricks cheating on their wives and girlfriends? Don't they all deserve what I give them?"

"Who named you judge, Clare? Can't you confront your uncle directly?"

"He's dead, probably had a heart attack fucking another kid. My father's dead, too. Mother's not worth the trouble. If not fuck me, who then? After all, they make the choice, don't they?"

"I'll call the police tonight, Clare. I'm sorry these terrible things happened to you, but what you're doing is to judge, then murder men."

"Call the law, Doc, you'll hear about judgment." I dialed the police phone number.

"Hello, Sargent Frazier please."

"Who's calling?"

"Dr. Armstrong." Murmurs.

"Hello, this is Sargent Frazier. What's the problem?"

"I wish to report a crime."

"Yeah, you do it?"

"No, not me."

"Who then?"

"A patient."

"What's the crime?"

"Attempted murder."

"OK, go on."

"The patient is a high priced courtesan with HIV. She does not divulge her infection to her clients nor insist on adequate protection, like a condom."

"Who are the dicks?"

"I don't know, she won't supply names."

"So you don't know any specific dicks who might have been infected?"

"No."

"Uh-huh. Any complaints from the dicks?"

"No."

"Do you know of any dicks—I assume we're talking guys, right?—who got AIDS from this bitch?"

"No, no specific man."

"So, Doc, we just have her story, nothing else?"

"Just this story. But really, officer, if she passes this disease to these men, it's a death sentence."

"Yeah, right, Doc. So you got nothing, no witness, no harmed party, not even a dick's black book. Just a whore's story. I can't do anything with this. What do you want, anyway?"

"You could investigate."

"You know what I got here? A desk full of real crimes, murders, assaults. Real victims, not some whore's tale of giving a dumb dick his due. Find out more, Doc. Get specific, or don't waste my time."

Thursday night was a traffic jam of the sick and desperate. Two hours sleep, a long day of problems and patients on my mind, I entered Clare's room for her final discharge talk. Betty was combing Clare's long hair and chaplain Peter had left his phone number on the bedside stand. The nurse was going over the discharge details.

"So, the good doctor appears under the weather, bad night?"

"Yeah, bad night, Doctor Clare. You OK to go home?"

"I'm ready. You have some great people here. I think they really care about me. That hasn't happened for a long time. How'd your police call go?"

"You were right. The sheriff was mostly irritated that I was wasting his time."

"So, you see, Doc, no one cares. No one will stop me and neither can you."

"Think about what you're doing, Clare. The lives you're entering and destroying. And for what? The sin of lust?"

"Bye, Doc, and thanks for everything, but get some sleep for God's sake. You look terrible."

Two months later Clare returned to the ER DOA. Her roommate, Crystal, was in the family waiting room, exhausted and anxious as before.

"What happened, Crystal?"

"She tried to go back to our old ways. Weird, demanding, rich fuckers, their way or the highway. But her hate was no longer strong enough to keep her going. And when the hate was less, there was only sadness. She insisted the men use condoms. They got very angry and some left. Drugs finally overwhelmed her. The whole fucking mess. She hadn't used heroin for months. It was so easy and for awhile brought relief. She asked me to thank you, Betty, the nurses, and Peter. It's funny isn't it? A little kindness did her in."

I left the family room, my spirits low. Had I contributed to this poor woman's death? Could I have done more? Peter walked up and placed a hand on my shoulder and said, "Real sad, Jack. We did what we could. Her heart was too broken."

I turned to Peter and asked, "Is there some hope for her, Peter?"

Peter replied, "By insisting, even at the end, that the men use condoms, she was showing mercy, and Jesus said in the Sermon on the Mount, 'Blessed are the merciful for they shall obtain mercy.' And I believe in God's mercy."

Deb burst through the morgue door in a rush and said, "OK guys, this is sad news, yes, but are we responsible for their whole screwed up lives by just doing our jobs and lending a hand? Doc, let's move. There are critical patients down the hall who need help now!"

VOICES

Oscar's dry lips curled downward as he refused to go to radiology for his CAT scan.

"Do you think I'm a pin cushion, Doc?" he growled.

Oscar lay back in the automated hospital bed, the room dull white, bare of any personal touch. No get-well cards cluttered the bedside stand. The blood pressure cuff dangled awkwardly from the wall hanger, left quickly by the evening nurse who stormed from the room after Oscar's last verbal jab.

Oscar's long finger pointed at me from the end of his thin arm, "So what now, Doc? No ideas? When is the kind and experienced Dr. Koffman coming back? I'm not ready for the ground yet!" he growled.

"He'll be gone another week, Mr. Carter. You'll have to deal with me," I said. I was a young, thirty-four-year-old physician covering for my senior partner's large medical practice while he attended a medical conference. Oscar was both his neighbor and long-term patient, a retired mechanical engineer. Oscar's wife had died the year before after a long and draining illness. His children distant, physically and emotionally, Oscar withdrew to his study, venturing out only for necessary shopping and to work silently in his yard. His home became as dreary as Oscar's mourning face.

At first Oscar's weight loss seemed a likely result of his depression. But then the weight loss accelerated and was accompanied by a deep, boring epigastric pain that tightened his jaws and drained his pale face. He hid his illness like his grief until he appeared in the emergency room one Sunday afternoon. A preliminary evaluation failed to find the specific cause of his pain; he was transferred to a medical room for additional evaluation, which he initially contested. Sunday night, his pain returned, and his heart raced and skipped. The monitor beeped and the night nurse, Jenny, appeared.

"You okay, Oscar?" Her eyes focused on Oscar, then the flickering monitor.

"My guts are busting, honey. Where the hell's my pain medication? You girls watching TV again?" he jabbed.

As Jenny flashed with anger and left the room to retrieve his morphine, she whispered, "He's all yours, Doc. Good luck with this bastard."

I sat down next to his bed. Ten p.m. and the road only half travelled.

"Look, Oscar, we've got to move along. The morphine takes your pain away, but we need to find out why you have the pain," I reasoned.

Oscar smirked and said, "All you young doctors want to do is tests and more tests. You getting a piece of the action, Doc?"

I sighed, but Oscar jabbed again. "Move along, Jack, you must have more important patients to see."

Oscar's innuendo and condescension brought anger to my lips, which was stymied by the urgent buzzing of my pager.

"I'll be back tomorrow, Oscar. We *will* talk some more," I sparred.

The next day rushed by, a Monday clinic full of familiar, friendly, and cooperative patients. The routine softened the irritation I felt from the preceding night. With clinic over, I drove slowly back to the hospital, rehearsing how to convince Oscar to go along with tests he needed but was resisting. Without family support he depended on the trust I had to somehow summon. As I reached the third floor stairwell, my pager came to life. "Code blue, room 316." Oscar's room! I sprinted up the stairs, then down the hall, reaching Oscar's room simultaneously with the code nurse and respiratory therapist. The cardiac monitor display was chaotic— ventricular fibrillation. No breath escaped from Oscar's mouth, no pulse was detectable in his neck. The crash cart banged into the room.

"Let's shock him now," I called to the RN, Jennifer, who was charging the defibrillator. We cranked the defibrillator up to 360 joules, pressed the pads to Oscar's thin chest, and shocked him not once, but three times. The respiratory therapist slid the endotracheal tube in on the first try. I had more trouble placing the central intravenous catheter in Oscar's chest, probably because of hypotension. Finally, on the second try, the catheter hit the vein, and a series of IV medications were infused. The third defibrillator shock worked, and Oscar's heart shifted back to a normal rhythm. The code culminated after thirty minutes.

We took Oscar to the ICU where he did surprisingly well. We weaned him from the ventilator and life support on the third day. He was transferred back to the medical ward and his old room. At first, Oscar was apathetic and confused; slowly he became oriented and cooperative. His tests were completed, showing a small heart attack which had led to his cardiac arrest. The abdominal CAT scan showed an inoperable, metastatic, pancreatic cancer.

"He's different somehow," Jenny reflected. "He goes along with tests. He even thanked me for bringing a new pillow this morning. What gives?" she questioned.

I thanked Jenny for her perseverance. Evening rounds were late, the day lapsing into twilight. The Blue Ridge Mountains were visible through Oscar's window. I sat down at his bedside. We discussed his heart attack, the cancer, his prognosis, pain control, talking with his family, and the details of his discharge plan. Finally, a thin hand signaled a stop. His grey-blue eyes looked up to mine.

"You know, Doc, I saw it all," he commented.

"Saw what, Oscar?"

"I saw you shock me not once, but three times. The young guy slipped that breathing thing into my throat on the first try. Slick. That IV in my chest was tough, huh? You looked upset when it didn't go in the first time, but you did okay the second time." He smiled, not a smirk now.

"Were you awake the whole time, Oscar?"

"No, Doc, I was up there." He pointed to the southeast corner of the room, next to the window.

"I watched for awhile. Then I began to drift and float into the darkness. I was frightened at first, but the air was warm, and I could see a faint, distinct light that seemed to be drifting toward me. Then it began. Oh, the voices, the murmuring voices," he spoke with reverence.

"Did you hear us talking during the code, Oscar?"

"Yes, but the murmurs were not you, but all the folks I'd loved and lost: my wife, my brother, my friends who have passed on. The murmur of voices was like a soft chorus—kind, familiar, and welcoming," he related.

"Did you want to join them, Oscar?"

"Oh, yes, I did. But then you pulled me back. I hovered over my body for awhile. I could see the three of you working feverishly. Suddenly, I was back inside, a second of awareness, then darkness. Then there was the world, a blur at first, then clearing. I awoke," he said.

"Do you feel strong enough to go home soon? Should I call your son?"

"I'm weak physically, Doc, but I know what I have to do. There is so little time. I have amends to make. Thank you! Oh, thank you for this chance!" He reached for my hand for a moment. "I'll be okay now," he smiled.

Oscar left the hospital the next day. His son returned to Winchester to help care for his father in his last weeks and wept at his funeral. So did I.

THE LAST CHILD

Gordon sat uneasily in the red leather chair, hunched over across from my wide, old, oak desk, his body framed by the filtered light of a fading autumn day. The chair was reserved for serious medical conversations between doctor and patient; comfortable and a bit worn on the arm rests, the red chair had held many souls receiving news of cancer and AIDS, and some experiencing the deep sigh of relief that the shadow on the x-ray or the recently palpated abdominal lump was not cancer, but something benign. Today though, the conversation belonged to Gordon, who wanted to be sure I understood his and his wife's wishes regarding end-of-life care.

"I'm tired, Doc. I'm like an old truck that can barely move even though it's just received a tune-up. Estace and I talked about this last weekend and we filled out the Advance Directive papers your nurse gave us. And you'll be proud of me, I even called two of the kids and told them what we've decided," Gordon said.

Gordon was a seventy-eight-year-old independent farmer. He had worked hard his entire life running the farm and doing much of the manual labor himself. He knew about life and death from the farm where his cows, pigs, and chickens acted out the cycle of life in an accelerated fashion. His arms and legs were muscular, tanned, and lined, but even at rest, if watched closely, you could observe Gordon's rapid respiratory rate trying to compensate for his compromised lung function. Gordon had smoked one or at times two packs of unfiltered cigarettes per day since his forties, and now suffered from advanced pulmonary emphysema.

"Now look, Doc, I know the end is just around the corner. I filled out your forms, but between you and me, when the sun sets you just let me fade out, too. We're straight on this?" Gordon stated.

"Yes, Gordon, I understand. Should we bring Estace back to be sure she agrees and understands as well?" I asked.

"OK. And my daughter, Ginny, is here too," Gordon added.

Estace was plain, lined by age and toil, but crisply dressed, as was Ginny. Both women preferred to stand as we discussed Gordon's condition and end-of-life preferences.

"So we're in agreement?" I asked the taut threesome.

"Damn it, Gordon Garrison," Estace finally hissed. "We wouldn't be here in this fancy office if you hadn't been hooked on those weeds! Now we'll be stuck out on that farm with the animals and no able-bodied man to lend a hand."

Gordon had slipped so far into the old red chair that they seemed as one. No hand extended to Gordon's slumped shoulders, nor did arms embrace him in this final sadness. I let the silence linger.

"Any further questions?" I asked.

"No, Doctor. Seems perfectly clear to me," Estace responded.

"How do the other children feel? Have you shared this decision with them?" I asked.

"Gordon talked to both our sons. Paul and Matthew live in DC now. Don't come home much. He," Estace began, pointing a long finger at Gordon, "makes them work. But, yes, they understand. No problem there."

Gordon finally looked up as if just awakened from a deep slumber.

"How about Rosie?" he asked.

Estace scoffed. "If she cared, she'd have come home for your birthday," Estace replied.

"California is a long way off. I think we should at least call and talk to her," Gordon offered.

"You go ahead, Gordon. I've washed my hands of that girl. You spoiled her because she was our last child," Estace scolded.

Gordon sighed but answered, "She's our fourth child. Went to college in California and married a doctor. Smart kid. She rebelled against us though and Estace never let up. Rosie lives in San Francisco and works for the university." Gordon's pride shone in his eyes, as did the hostility radiating from Estace. Ginny shifted uneasily.

"I'll call her for you, Daddy, if you wish," Ginny offered.

Gordon smiled slightly and nodded at Ginny.

"OK, Gordon, you've done a lot of work here. Be sure to give a copy of your wishes to each of your children and your attorney, and I'll keep a copy. You keep an original and bring it with you if you need to come to the hospital. Ginger, my nurse, will call in your prescription. And congratulations on giving up smoking!" I summarized.

Gordon slowly lifted out of the red chair, looked at Estace and Ginny, and nodded at the door.

"Comfortable chair, Doc. And thanks for the time," Gordon said.

Several months passed. While I was away at a medical conference, Gordon was admitted to Winchester Medical Center with pneumonia and worsening shortness of breath. My young partner, Avery, took care of Gordon in my absence. Checking out the hospital patient census on Friday evening for a weekend call, Avery was pessimistic about Gordon.

"He's pretty weak, Jack. Not a lot of margin left in those old lungs. He's on antibiotics, steroids, and oxygen. Just about everything I could think of, but a ventilator and the ICU. The family was pretty clear about not wanting life support and the ICU. The wife did most of the talking. Gordon seemed a little depressed, but hard to be certain when he's so weak."

Avery was the consummate internal medicine physician—careful, thoughtful, a bee on a flower about details. He had studied Russian literature in college at Duke, not because he thought it was useful, but because he found Russian culture interesting.

Avery sat up in the old red chair and cleared his throat, as he often did when about to say something serious. His young face and thick, blond hair made him appear like a teenage boy.

"You know, Jack, he might be able to beat this pneumonia, but he's probably going to need an ICU stay and ventilatory support for a while," he offered.

When Avery got to the ventilatory support, his voice trailed off so that you could hardly hear the words, a habit he had acquired of pronouncing controversial statements in a whisper, as if words spoken softly would be easier to accept.

"Good point, Avery. It may come to that decision, but Gordon seems ready for an end. Keep an eye open for the California daughter if she flies in. I've not met her or been allowed to call her," I said.

The phone rang at 10 p.m. Friday night. Hospital Nurse Elizabeth apologized for calling late.

"We have a real problem here, Doctor Armstrong. It's Mr. Garrison. He's been failing all day. Dr. Gibbs was in earlier and suggested moving him to the ICU with intubation and ventilation, but he and his wife both said no, that they had talked this over with you, and he was ready if the end was near. But then their last child from California arrived, and oh boy did things change!" Elizabeth said. Elizabeth was that rare combination of intelligence and kindness that made for a perfect nurse. Avery elaborated.

"Yeah, Jack, you warned me about the last child, the one who didn't know what was going on. She flew into the room just as I was summarizing letting Gordon go. She is very different from the rest of the family. Attractive, long blond hair, vivacious, tanned, and opinionated. She just walked right by her mother, sister, and me and reached down and hugged her father, kissed him on the cheek, and said how great it was to see him again. Then she turned to her mother and sister and said, "Daddy and I have some things to discuss, alone."

"If looks could have killed, Mrs. Garrison would have slain us all right on the spot. The last child looked at Gordon, and he nodded at the door and out went Ginny and Estace. I asked if they wanted me to stay, but she, Rosie, said no; they needed to talk alone for awhile, and to be honest, I was glad to walk out," Avery whispered, completing checkout. Elizabeth continued.

"So Rosie sits on the side of the bed and talks and laughs with Mr. Garrison for over an hour. Then it's time for his breathing treatment, and Dave, the respiratory therapist, takes over, and she flies out as quick as she flew in. After the treatment is over, he's a little bit better, and he calls me in. He says, "Elizabeth, my daughter Rosie and I have talked things over, and I've changed my mind. I think I want to keep going." After he said that, he closed his eyes. "She's really something isn't she, our last child?" Then he just falls asleep. At that exact moment my beeper went off, and Mr. Franklin down the hall had just vomited a whole basin of blood. I didn't have time to linger, and I ran off down the hall," Elizabeth exclaimed.

"Did you meet the last child, Elizabeth?" I asked.

"Just briefly, Dr. Armstrong. As Dave and I entered the room to set up the breathing treatment, she was there for a moment. She said, "I have to go now Daddy." She had been crying. She leaned over and kissed Mr. Garrison, and said "I love you." Mr. Garrison teared up a bit too, then she was gone," Elizabeth stated.

"What's going on now, Elizabeth?" I asked.

"Well, as I said, after the breathing treatment he seemed a little better. But as the night progressed, he became weaker and then lethargic. Dave got an arterial blood gas, and Mr. Garrison was really retaining carbon dioxide. I guess the end is near," Elizabeth added.

Our lungs act as large bellows, inhaling oxygen and expiring carbon dioxide, the byproduct of human metabolism. If carbon dioxide accumulates because of muscle weakness or lung failure, the chemical gas acts as a sedative, depressing further both cerebral and respiratory function, eventually leading to respiratory arrest and death.

"Everything on the chart says let him go. And now his wife and daughter are here saying that they'd all agreed on what to do, but I told them about their last child's visit, and that Mr. Garrison said he'd changed his mind and wanted to keep going!" Elizabeth's voice rose with emotion as she pronounced he wanted to keep going.

"But the wife said, 'Damm her,' and stormed out of the room. They're behind me, sitting on the hall floor crying," Elizabeth said.

"Can you keep Gordon going until I can drive in? I'll be about ten minutes," I requested.

"Yes. Dave's here, and we're giving Mr. Garrison another breathing treatment. What are we going to do?" Elizabeth concluded, and hung up.

As I arrived at Gordon' room, Estace and Ginny were talking in hushed tones just down the hall from the door entrance. I greeted them, but they averted their eyes, then just pointed at the room, as if to say, he's all yours now. Elizabeth and I walked to the bedside where Dave was slowly assisting Gordon's breathing with the IPPB machine.

Dave was a quiet, deeply religious man with a kind face and strong hands.

"This treatment isn't doing much. The dilemma is, what do we do next?" Dave asked.

"Did Gordon confide in you, Dave?" I asked.

"No, Doc. I guess this is true carbon dioxide narcosis," Dave replied.

"Well, Dave, I guess we need to bring him up and ask him at this moment what he wishes us to do," I said.

Dave smiled slightly and said, "And how are we going to do that without the ventilator?"

"Put in your oral airway and let's hyperventilate him with the Ambu bag until we blow off enough carbon dioxide for him to wake up. Then maybe, if we're real lucky, he'll be clear enough to give us guidance," I offered.

Dave neatly slipped in the oral airway, repositioned Gordon's neck, and attached the Ambu bag. Instead of ten respirations per minute we cycled Gordon with thirty breaths per minute. After thirty minutes, Gordon's eyes fluttered and he began to stir.

"Gordon, can you hear me?" I asked.

"Yeah, Doc. I hear you. Boy, was I asleep!" Gordon exclaimed.

"Where are you, Gordon?" I asked.

"I'm in the hospital," Gordon replied.

"Do you know who is with you here at the bedside, Gordon?" I asked.

Gordon's hands slowly rubbed his eyes as if it were early morning, and the chickens needed to be fed.

"Ah, you're trying to trick me, Doc. That's Elizabeth, my sweet nurse, and Dave, my breathing buddy. You should get to know the young people," Gordon coughed, then laughed softly at his own joke.

"Gordon, I hear your last child visited you from California today, and you had a long talk. Did you change your mind about what you'd like us to do to help you?" I asked.

"Ah, ain't she great? You'll have to meet her. So full of life and love. She said she hoped I'd hang on for awhile so we could spend some time together and help the family mend. I guess I agree with her," he said.

"So you want us to press on, Gordon? Ventilator and the ICU, OK?" I asked.

"I know this is a big change, Doc, but yeah, do whatever is necessary."

Gordon slowly adjusted the oxygen prongs in his nose, sighed, then laid back on his pillow asleep, his strength now depleted.

We intubated Gordon, moved him to the ICU, and supported his respirations with a ventilator. Gradually the pneumonia cleared, and Gordon's breathing improved. He was weaned off the ventilator, left the ICU after five days, and made a slow but steady recovery. The split family visited Gordon at separate times. Given Gordon's precarious condition, I arranged for him to return to Selma, my private office, in seven days.

Gordon sat quietly in the red leather chair, the oxygen tank on his left and the last child sitting on his right. The room had a slight floral aroma drifting from the brightly attired young woman who was leaning toward Gordon and holding his right hand in hers. After we discussed his condition, treatment, and activity level, the last child rose and helped Gordon gently to his feet.

"Isn't he a fighter, Doctor? We really need him to help our family mend." She smiled at Gordon, gave me a small hug, and said, "Thank you for giving us our Dad back."

Gordon lived two additional years, weak but alert. The family healed slowly with his help. He died peacefully at home.

LION IN THE NIGHT

Chad had stroked the winning cross-court forehand, classic form, honed in prep school, then on the tennis courts in college. He strode to the net, blond hair unruffled and untainted by grey, even at forty-five years of age. Chad pointed his expensive Prince racquet at his discouraged and beaten male opponent, kissed his pretty female partner, then his equally attractive female opponent.

"Nice try, guys, better luck next time," he quipped.

Chad waved to the few spectators, gathered to drink a few beers and watch the final Stonebrook Racquet Club mixed doubles tennis match. Although the match was just a Winchester, Virginia small-town affair, he viewed every public appearance as a Chad opportunity.

"Not much competition for you, Chad," said Ed, his friend and frequent tennis partner. Chad was a traveling salesman, no office or staff. His friends were those he cultivated for social and business purposes. No seed was planted randomly.

"Where are your girls, Chad?" asked Ed.

"Darlene took them to the Smithsonian for Linda's birthday. They won't miss me—I gave them the plastic. Besides, they insisted on going to Mass and I wasn't going to screw up my game by setting the alarm at 6 a.m. so I could listen to a bunch of priestly hocus-pocus. Life is right here, right now, Ed." Chad pointed his tennis racquet around the courts.

As he gestured, Chad's clear blue eyes roamed, then settled on, a trim, dark-haired beauty.

"Careful, Chad. That's Jean—Jack's wife," Ed murmured.

"Ha, Doctor Jack! There's a guy who's never around, always working at the hospital, missing all the fun, including this tournament. If Jean was my wife, she'd be locked up in the bedroom."

"Don't you have an appointment soon with Jack, Chad?"

"Yeah, Darlene's flipping out. And Vince, my doc, thinks I've got TB in the neck. Something he called 'Scrofula.' He's so old school. All I've really got is this little lump in my neck. I told Darlene and Vince not to sweat the small stuff, but they made a rush appointment anyhow. Hey, are we going to play in that Middleburg match next week? I know a couple sales reps who really swing that could make the weekend Love–40!"

"Tennis, yes. Girls, no! I screwed up my first marriage that way. This one's a keeper," Ed replied.

Chad waved to the thinning crowd, winked at Jean, and jogged after Ed, confident, certain.

Later Sunday night at the dinner party of a prominent local businessman, Chad stepped out on the second-story porch overlooking the lake and clear night. He inhaled a full drag of smoke, leaned against the porch rail, and gazed up at the stars. Jack, his future physician, stood a few feet away: same height, but thinner, same blue eyes, but ringed by dark circles, now focused directly on Chad.

"Can you believe we're here, Jack? These are big-time people. The real insiders," Chad said.

"They're just people like you and me, Chad, trying to stay afloat and find a path through the woods." Over half the collected party were also Jack's patients.

"I bet we could get some real financial and medical advice right in that room, Jack."

"Free financial and medical advice are worth about the same. Be careful, Chad."

The following Monday evening Chad was perched on Jack's exam table, shirt on the chair, shifting nervously, out of his element.

Jack examined Chad head to toe but returned to the supraclavicular fossa, the shallow space above the anterior chest, between the shoulders and the neck. The left supraclavicular fossa received the lymph flow from the chest, and swollen lymph nodes could be a harbinger of a hidden chest disease. Jack's fingertips lingered on the firm mass, fixed and hard, in the left supraclavicular fossa. Jack asked Chad to dress and meet next door in his office. The office was quiet, with two wood-framed windows and a wooden floor crafted from an 1840 home.

Chad began the conversation, "Mind if I smoke?"

"Probably not a good idea."

Chad slid the cigarette pack back in this upper shirt pocket. "OK, Jack. What's the score?"

"The lump in your neck could be TB like Vince thought, but it feels malignant. We need a CAT scan and a biopsy right away."

"I'm playing in a tennis tournament this week and attending an important business trip next week."

"Your CAT scan is in the morning, and the biopsy is scheduled in two days. I called the surgeon while you were dressing. Forget the tournament, Chad. This is important."

"You know, Jack, you're too serious. Lighten up. How bad could it be?"

"Bad and serious. Bring Darlene with you next week for a report on your tests."

"All right. I'll go along; but no, I won't bring Darlene and not a word from you. I'll take care of this myself!"

Chad had the CAT scan and biopsy. His lung cancer was in the apex (top of the chest) of the left lung, the supraclavicular mass was a metastatic lymph node. Chad was started on radiation therapy and chemotherapy, surgery and a cure not an option.

Therapy was exhausting, but Chad continued his relentless pace of work, travel, and tennis. He gave up smoking, but avoided a discussion of prognosis despite offers from his oncologist and radiation therapist. Darlene became depressed and reclusive as Chad's weight slipped weekly. Darlene confided in Jack's wife, Jean, that she had a sense Chad was failing; but he refused to discuss his treatment other than to say the chemo made him sick. He couldn't stand the sight of food; and when chemo was over, he'd be back at it.

Finally, pneumonia brought Chad down. The high fever and shortness of breath pushed Chad's frail body to the edge, and then to the hospital.

Jack's breakfast was at 6 a.m., hospital rounds beginning early. The children were asleep. Jean sat at the table with Jack. They tried never to miss a meal together.

"So you're Chad's doctor now? He has cancer, not TB. How did this happen?"

"Well, he doesn't talk or trust easily. He shuts up with both the oncologist and the radiation docs and won't see Vince because Vince told him it was probably TB. I guess I'm the one he'll talk to because he beats me soundly in tennis."

"You know he doesn't confide in Darlene. Around Stone-brook he chases anything with a skirt. We call him 'Bad Chad.' Now he's all yours."

"I don't think he'll last long. He's terrified of death and death is soon."

"You know, Jack, you can't fix everyone and everything. He's made his own death bed."

"He doesn't have to die so alone."

Chad lay in the white-sheeted hospital bed, picking at the sheets. Darlene and Elizabeth, the night medical nurse, tried to comfort him, offering pillows, water, and medication. Chad's agitation was contagious; his anxious breath was the room's palpable aroma. As his pneumonia subsided and his mental status cleared, he realized he would die very soon. He had developed Cheyne-Stokes respirations, a central brain-controlled, rhythmic, and terminal breathing pattern, during which the respiratory rate accelerates then declines, finally stopping completely. Cessation of respiration, or apnea, can last thirty seconds or more and terminates with a deep gasp. With each cycle, Chad became more frightened, as did Darlene and Elizabeth. Darlene confided she felt Chad was dying over and over again with each cycle. Their joint apprehension and fatigue hovered over the room like a low-lying, threatening cloud cover before a storm. I entered the room at 10 p.m., the end of hospital evening rounds.

"How's it going tonight, Chad?" Jack asked.

"Oh, it's terrible, Jack. Just awful. First, I feel as if I can't catch my breath. Then, without willing it, I breathe faster, then slower, then, oh my God, I stop—and I feel myself falling away, dropping into a deep, dark pit."

"Are you alone as you fall?"

"That's the worst part. I can see Darlene and the girls inside our home and it's light and warm and familiar, but they don't see me. It's as if I'm invisible or already gone! Then I start falling away into the dark pit. Oh, it's so cold. I begin to shiver. I try to call out, but I have no voice. I think I'm falling into hell without a hand to hold me.

"Do you want me to stay awhile?"

"Yes, yes! That would be great."

Darlene slowly stood up, kissed Chad's forehead, and leaned over to whisper to Jack as she turned to the door.

"I can't take it another minute. He's terrified! I feel I'm being pulled into the grave with him. I've got to go home to be with the kids."

Elizabeth waved Jack out of the room. "I'd like to stay. It's so sad, but I've got a whole floor of patients to look after." "Good luck, Doc."

Chad's breathing accelerated, slowed, and stopped in predictable cycles. He refused morphine as he felt he needed to stay awake to "settle some things." As the night progressed, anxiety passed from Chad to anyone entering the room, including Jack. Jack sat at the bedside, the room warm, the infusion pump's beep the only audible intrusion. He drifted into a deep slumber, dreaming he was back in his childhood bed in Detroit. The wind was howling and shadows were dancing outside the bedroom window and on the walls of the room. Occasionally a tree would bend and creak, and Jack would burrow his five-year-old body deep into the pillows and covers.

"Mom, Mom!" he called out.

Up the stairs came the familiar pad of feet. She sat on the edge of his bed. "What's wrong, Jack?"

"There's something outside trying to get me!"

"It's just the wind and trees, Jack. Try to go to sleep."

"But it sounds like monsters on the trees and they're trying to come in the windows."

"There are scary noises tonight, Jack, but you're lucky to have Lion here to protect you. Here, Jack, put Lion under your arm. No monster would dare to come close to you."

She tucked the big stuffed lion under Jack's arm, pulled the covers to his chin, and kissed his cheek.

"Be brave, Jack. With Lion you'll be safe."

Jack awoke abruptly to Chad's shrill yell in the night. "Oh, no. That was the worst yet. Darlene and the girls disappeared as I fell. I was so cold and alone. I know I'm dying, Jack. Don't let me fall asleep again."

"You're OK now, Chad. I'll wake you if you stop breathing."

"OK. God, forgive me. I've been such a shit. I've only thought about myself, my job, my tennis, my status, me, me, me. Darlene and the kids must hate me!"

"I think they all love you, but you've kept them at a distance."

"I have to try to show I care, but I'm so weak."

"They're coming in this morning, Chad. Tell them you love them. I think it will help them, too. Will you talk to your priest later today as well?"

"Yes, yes," Chad wept with a sob. "I'll give it my last strength."

"After you've talked with Darlene, the girls, and your priest, I'd like to give you some morphine to help you rest. It's been a long night. Will you be ready tonight?"

"I'm so tired. I hope they can forgive me. But, yes, I'll be ready."

Chad and Darlene and the three girls talked most of the day. They remembered fun vacations, silly moments, and watching *The Hulk* on TV while sharing popcorn. Darlene cried, told Chad she loved him, and yes, she forgave him. They left the room as the priest slipped in to hear Chad's final confession.

Chad accepted morphine that night. His breathing remained rhythmic but peaceful until it ceased.

LAST WORDS

Cyril's kind eyes were framed by deep, dark circles. A geriatric specialist, the many demands and problems of his aging patients were rarely fixed for long, drawing on his patience and knowledge to ease the last years of their lives. Cyril was the final physician of six to check out for weekend call, a necessary, but tedious ritual.

"Well, I guess that's about it, except for Earl. He's a sad one. Bright engineer. Worked hard his whole life, until Parkinson's disease grabbed him. He's really gone downhill the last six months. Stiff as a board. He can't swallow any more. He's lost fifty pounds this year," Cyril explained with a sigh.

"Why was he admitted this time, Cyril?" I asked.

"Dehydration and pneumonia. He aspirates every time he eats. Pathetic to see such a strong guy fade," he elaborated.

"How much are we doing?" I asked.

"The neurologists have signed off. I talked to his wife and children last month and again today. They requested we stop the antibiotics and just keep Earl comfortable. They're ready to let him go. He hasn't spoken for three days," Cyril stated.

"Is he a DNR?"

"Yeah, no point in coding the guy now. The sooner he goes, the better. The advance directions are on the chart, all signed. Pretty straightforward, really. I think he'll go this weekend. They shouldn't bother you," Cyril explained. We both knew the end of life, like the beginning, was chancy; the end drama often determined by who was at the bedside.

Hospital rounds were long, but uneventful that Friday. Earl's devoted wife, Ellen, tended his silent bedside. Cyril had slipped in after dinner to stop the antibiotics and offer a sympathetic ear.

Saturday morning started early with an ICU Code Blue and cardiac arrest. After the code the demonic beeper buzzed like an angry bee whose hive had been breached: patients storming the emergency room, calls for consultation, nurses needing orders clarified, apprehensive families visiting ill relations who "just wish for a moment to know where we stand," spiking fevers, and falling blood pressures all buzzing for attention.

Late morning I arrived at Earl's room. Thin and unresponsive, his face a mask of passivity, Earl lay still. Earl had been a successful engineer and in spite of his profound disability, had retained his intelligence. Elizabeth, his primary nurse, had cared for him for several days. She had bathed and fed him, but also had been present for the family meetings with Cyril. She was comfortable with his pending demise.

"He seems to be resting quietly now. No response, even with turning, since Thursday. Dr. Barch stopped the antibiotics last night. His temperature is 103 degrees and his blood pressure is low. Won't be long now, Doc," Elizabeth said.

"Family OK with his care?" I asked.

"Yes, they visit daily. 'Just keep him comfortable,' they say. They leave early, but his wife stays by his bedside late. She's very devoted, but also emotional. Cries a lot. Married forty-five years. Can you imagine that? Married longer than I am old!" she exclaimed.

"Any other issues tonight, Elizabeth?" I asked.

"Well, we, the nurses, don't understand why we're keeping the IVs going. Seems to be just drawing out the end. And we have to stick him with needles a lot. Got to hurt," she emphasized.

"What does the family say?" I replied.

"They brought it up themselves last night when the IV came out again. He sort of grimaced when we stuck him," she said.

"OK, let's stop the IVs. No more needle sticks or phlebotomy," I answered.

The day continued on, consumed with the living or those who still had a shot at life. At last, at 7 p.m., I walked through the front door of my home. Chessie, our Shelty dog, saluted me with a bark and a lick. Liz, my teenage daughter and devoted soccer player, looked up from her homework.

"Hi, Dad. Some long day," she stated.

"Yeah, long day, but fun Monday," I replied.

"Fun for you, Coach, you don't have to run the laps," she joked about our joint soccer practices, usually on Monday and Thursday nights.

Together the phone rang and the angry beeper buzzed. My wife, Jean, kissed me and pointed to supper on the kitchen table.

"I'd better get this, Jean," I stated.

"How about a little food first?" she suggested.

"I think the phone and the beeper are the same person. Let me see what they want," I parried.

"What's up, Elizabeth?" I asked, turning off the beeper.

"I'm working a double tonight, Dr. Armstrong. I should have gone home. But listen." She held the phone up to the room. I could hear Ellen crying in the background.

"Is that Earl's wife? What's happened?" I asked.

"Oh, it's just terrible. She's been like this for thirty minutes," Elizabeth whispered.

"Is Earl dying now?" I asked.

"No, actually, he hasn't changed much since this morning. But a priest is here. I don't recognize him. I don't think he's from Winchester. He's younger than the family priest and he's very upset. He wants to talk to you right now!" she stammered.

"Are you Dr. Armstrong, the treating physician?" the priest asked with authority.

"Yes, I am," I replied.

"Did you stop Earl's antibiotics and intravenous fluids today?" he cross-examined me.

"Yes, I did. Earl is dying. His Parkinson's disease has run its course. There is nothing further we can do to halt his neurological decline. His family made the decision with Dr. Barch to provide comfort and support only," I explained.

"But if you continued the antibiotics and fluids, Earl might survive to live another day, right?" he countered.

"That is not the point, Father. The family doesn't wish him to receive additional treatment that might cause him only to linger and suffer more. Comfort only, they requested," I explained, now angry.

"This is against the teachings of the church, Doctor. I have told Mrs. Chadry that Earl cannot receive the last rites nor pass to heaven under these circumstances," he insisted.

"Listen, Father, this is not your decision! You are interfering where you are not welcome. Do not leave that room! I am coming back to the hospital now," I replied sharply.

"I guess no dinner," sighed Jean.

"Keep it warm, honey. Can you believe that guy putting Ellen in this moral predicament?" I asked.

"Poor woman. Didn't the pope recently die of Parkinson's and refuse artificial nutrition? Seems it was OK for him," she replied.

I drove faster than usual during the six-minute trip to the hospital, then up three flights of stairs to Earl's room. Waiting outside the room was a very tired Nurse Elizabeth and hospital chaplain Peter Tarus.

"What do you think, Elizabeth?" I asked.

"Mrs. Chadry's beside herself. She had her mind made up as did Earl. Then the priest told her Earl was going to hell! She doesn't know what to do," Elizabeth explained.

"Where's the priest?" I asked.

"He left right after he hung up the phone with you. He seemed a bit afraid, really," she related.

"What do you think, Peter?" I asked the Quaker chaplain.

"This is unfair. The priest should have been here to provide comfort, not doubt and discord. He seemed uncaring and smug. As a Quaker, this question of letting a patient die naturally is not an issue for us," he explained.

"Did you talk to Ellen, Peter?" I asked.

"She just keeps rocking back and forth in the chair, crying and asking, 'Oh, what to do? I wish Earl was awake so he could help me make the right decision.'"

"Have you reached the children, Elizabeth?" I asked.

"I've tried, but all I get are those damn answering machines," she responded.

"What about Earl?" I asked.

"His blood pressure is low and he hasn't responded now for a couple of days."

I walked into the darkened room. Mrs. Chadry was seated in the corner. The room smelled of sweat, disinfectant, and the strange aroma of fear. Earl lay quietly on his back, the oxygen tubing inserted in his nose, the detached intravenous tubing hanging from the metal IV pole.

"I'm sorry, Mrs. Chadry. What do you wish us to do?" I asked, as I reached for her hands.

"Oh, I just don't know. I thought we all had agreed. I do know what Earl wanted. We talked often. 'Don't let them just keep me alive,' he said. Oh, but I can't let him die with this cloud of doubt. No last rites, no sacrament. What can we do?" she pleaded.

"Should we try to talk to Earl?" I asked.

"He hasn't spoken for days, but yes, please try," she responded.

Mrs. Chadry, Elizabeth, Peter, and I walked to Earl's bedside. I pulled up a chair and held Earl's hand for a few minutes.

"Do you hear me, Earl?" I asked.

Earl's eyes slowly opened. He looked first at his wife, then back to me. He whispered softly, but loud enough for us all to hear. He squeezed my hand slightly. "You can let me go, Doc." His eyes closed and his frail hand released mine.

"Did you hear Earl, Mrs. Chadry?" I asked.

"Oh, yes, yes!" she exclaimed.

"Is it OK then to honor your decision to keep Earl comfortable?" I asked.

"Yes, it's alright now, I know we're doing what he wishes."

Earl never spoke again. We left the intravenous fluids and antibiotics off. The following morning, Cyril, the geriatric specialist, agreed to meet with a second, older priest, who reassured Mrs. Chadry that her decision was morally acceptable and consistent with church teachings, and that Earl would receive the sacrament of the last rites. Earl died peacefully the next day.

ROXIE

Her reddish brown face pressed against the cage, her friendly eyes, framed by rings of black hair, smiled. Her long tail wagged encouragement, and Jean and I were hooked. Roxie had been found running wild in Baltimore with her brother weeks before her fortunate encampment at the Charlestown Briggs Animal Shelter. After we passed parent assessment and suitability scrutiny, Roxie joined our family in rural Winchester.

Our home is situated on a wooded, one-acre lot midway up a curving cul-de-sac. The road was flanked on the north by a huge cow farm and on the south by a densely wooded hill. Roxie and I greeted each sunrise and sunset with a quarter-mile walk to the end of the cul-de-sac and back. Rabbits, deer, and squirrels frequented our walks and were an endless source of curiosity, barks, and short chases.

ROXIE

Roxie made friends easily and quickly. Partway up the cul-de-sac lived a retired couple, Patsy and Bud. Bud had Parkinson's, so he rarely walked the street except for an occasional shuffling venture to the mailbox and back. Patsy, however, was an adventurer and often made quick car trips to play cards, visit friends, or shop. Though tall and athletic in bearing, Patsy was frail from her advancing heart failure. Nevertheless, she often stopped by on her way home, pulling her Lincoln Town Car into our driveway to greet Roxie with affection, an ear rub, and a dog treat. They became tail-wagging friends.

Months after Roxie joined our family, my wife Jean was wracked by abdominal pain. The diagnosis was quickly established as advanced ovarian cancer requiring urgent surgery. Arrangements were made at Johns Hopkins Hospital, just two hours away though it seemed like a lifetime. Patsy volunteered to keep Roxie as the duration of our absence was uncertain. Patsy had the perfect dog backyard, a swimming pool enclosed by a four-foot-high wooden fence.

Roxie and I toured her backyard that autumn night. The fence seemed secure. The fence was too high for even my energetic, jumping dog to leap. With that detail settled, Jean and I headed off to Johns Hopkins the next morning.

The first night, Roxie and Patsy toured the backyard together, one end of the leash around Roxie's neck and the other end firmly in Patsy's hands. Yet Roxie tugged, yearned to be free, to run in the yard. The next night, Patsy released Roxie to bound about the yard. After two quick laps, Roxie found the fence's weak point, low to the ground, which allowed her to break the slat, slip under the fence, and into the darkening woods.

Patsy called Roxie to no avail. Eventually Patsy rolled out the Town Car to search Jones Road, a busy rural highway, and Stonebrook Subdivision, home to many interesting and new dogs. No Roxie appeared. Feeling a sense of rising anxiety, Patsy returned home, strode to the backyard, stood at the fence's weak point, and resumed her calls. Racing from the woods, Roxie returned to the fence gate, wagging her tail, and licking Patsy's face. Such fear but such relief! On subsequent nights, Roxie and Patsy strolled the backyard together, but Roxie was always on a leash. They also ate and slept together. Bud would rub Roxie's ears while watching television, whispering in his soft voice, "Good dog. Nice dog."

Jean's surgery was long and difficult, but successful. We returned to Winchester and Roxie returned home. Life resumed a certain rhythm as I returned to work at the Selma Medical Clinic and Winchester Medical Center. Chemotherapy started for Jean. Patsy continued her visits until the cold ice of winter grounded the Town Car.

February 2007 was a bitter and icy winter. The ice had formed over snow, making a sheet of frozen glass of Patsy's driveway and front yard. Many driveways went unplowed, and the wind and cold kept many older folks inside. Still Roxie and I bundled up and made our morning and evening forages together.

Late one Tuesday night we leaned into the eastern wind, the sun having just set, and headed up the cul-de-sac. The ice glistened and the wind howled. We then approached Patsy and Bud's home, up an ice ridge to the south. Roxie went into a fit of barks, pulling strongly on her leash.

I searched the woods for signs of retreating deer and rabbits but none appeared. Roxie went into a three-legged point, her nose directed not at the dark woods, but at Patsy's driveway. Not knowing what to expect, I let Roxie lead me across the crunching lake of ice to the edge of the driveway. Lying face down, ice pick in his outstretched hand, was Bud. Ten feet of ice was chipped away from the garage, the beginning of a path to the mailbox.

Roxie rushed to Bud's snow covered face and licked. As I approached, I could hear Bud's soft whisper, "Help me, please help me." Patsy slowly came out through the garage, and we lifted Bud up and shuffled inside. Bud's hands were cold, but his legs were strong. We helped Bud into the house where he collapsed into his lazy boy chair. A dog treat appeared and a trembling hand rubbed Roxie's proud head. Patsy clapped her hands together and said, "Oh Roxie, you are a lifesaver!"

FEVER

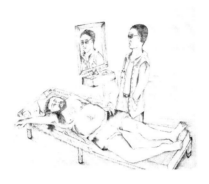

Ben was restless all night, a common occurrence since Vietnam. This night was different though, with drenching sweats and periodic, bone-rattling chills. Every muscle ached as if he'd chopped wood all day. Finally he gave up on sleep and wandered out to the kitchen of his handmade cedar cabin. When he returned from Vietnam, Ben found the company of civilians difficult and needed activity to divert his mind from the war. The cabin was a perfect outlet, heated by a huge stone fireplace and basic wood stove, equally illuminated by electric lights or oil lamps. He could exist off the grid if the apocalypse really came. He also had a gas water heater supplied by a propane tank. He drilled a well 400 feet deep next to the large garden of vegetables he planted each Spring. Ben was an independent soul.

Ben poured his black coffee, his left hand trembling a little from the high fever. His German Shepherd wandered over from his large bed and placed his jaw on Ben's leg, hoping for an early breakfast. The phone rang softly, loud noises not permitted in the quiet cabin. Ben knew it was his daughter, the only regular caller. His ex-wife lived in Gore, but let Ben take the initiative to make contact since the divorce. Ben was capable of going weeks with the dog, birds, and animals as his only companions. But his daughter was different. She understood his moods and also his strength. Ben could fix anything and often did when requested by other neighbors in the woods. She was calling this morning because she knew he had been ill, wasn't eating, and wasn't getting better. He finally picked up the phone.

"Hello, Dad. Are you better?"

"No, Jennifer. I feel like a dog left out in the rain all night."

"Let's go to the hospital, Dad."

"No. God, no, I'm not going back to that damn VA hospital. Four surgeries it took them to finally fix my leg from the bullet wound. I'll never trust those damn butchers again." Ben's voice rose as he pronounced "those damn butchers."

"Look, Dad, you're getting worse. I can tell by your voice. I have a very good doctor in Winchester: Dr. Barnes. Smartest guy I ever met. And nice, too. I'll pick you up at ten and he'll meet us in the emergency room. The VA will cover it because it's an emergency. Get dressed now, Dad. We *are* going!"

Ben hung up the phone. No one bossed him around but Jennifer. Ben was 6'4", 240 pounds of solid muscle. His beard and hair were dark brown and his blue eyes intense. He had scars on his right temple, the right side of his neck, and most of the length of his right leg. The Vietnam battle for survival had been personal and up close. Even his war buddies stayed away from the real war—horror, pain, and death, best left behind or at worst rediscovered in a dream world. Ben began to get dressed knowing Jennifer would be by in the next hour.

Dr. Barnes was making his usual dawn ICU rounds. He was a short, lean, hyperkinetic, serious, no-nonsense man. Board certified in internal medicine, pulmonary medicine, and intensive care, he was always accompanied by a tribe of learners, students, residents, pharmacists, and nurses. He had instructed the ER to call him immediately when Ben arrived; Jennifer and Ben's ex-wife, Pat, were both his private patients and favorites. When the call came, Dr. Barnes broke rounds, hustled down three flights of stairs, the elevator just too slow, followed by the young, scrambling tribe. He examined Ben thoroughly, diagnosed sepsis, probably originating in the abdomen, and began IV fluids and broad spectrum antibiotics. Three days and three nights passed. Ben's abdominal CAT was negative for an abscess and all his cultures were negative. Each night his temperature rose to 104 degrees followed by drenching sweats and shaking chills. One of the students suggested perhaps an infectious disease consult might be helpful. Dr. Barnes glared at the student, consultation a matter of pride, having to admit you might just need help figuring things out. Instead, Dr. Barnes harrumphed and ordered CT scans head to chest including the pelvis and retroperitonium. Finally, when all the scans were negative and the family anxiety was notably rising, he told the students to call me and request an ID consult.

It was late when I finally finished afternoon clinic. I shook Ben's hand and noted the tremor and the fact that he'd peeled off all his clothes but his shorts, preparing for his third shower of the day. As was my custom, I asked Ben why he thought Dr. Barnes had requested the consult.

Ben replied, "I said to Dr. Barnes, 'For God's sake, Doctor Barnes, I've been in here for three days and three nights. I'm just as sick as I was when I walked through the ER door. Dammit to hell, there must be some white-haired, nerdy doctor that you can call in to figure this out!'"

I looked across the room at the mirror over the patient sink. Could he really be referring to me? But the image looking back from the mirror was in fact an older man with white hair and deep, dark circles under his eyes, implying lots of experience, perhaps too much at times.

We settled in then, Ben hunched over the bedside table, sweat periodically breaking out on his face and arms. I asked Ben all the usual esoteric infectious disease questions, including illnesses in

Vietnam, blood transfusions around his numerous trauma surgeries, animal bites or scratches in the last two weeks, travel abroad, contact with friends or family recently returned from developing countries.

"Negative, Doctor. No to all these weird questions."

Ben's physical exam was remarkable for a temperature of 102 degrees, a pulse of 80, a slightly enlarged liver, and a subtly palpable and tender spleen in the left upper quadrant. As we wrapped up the exam, Jennifer walked in and asked Ben if he had told me about his hunting trip two weeks ago. Ben shrugged and asked if I thought the trip was relevant.

"Yes," I said. "Don't hold back. Tell me all the details of the trip."

Ben shot a deer and several squirrels, all of which he prepared in the wild. One deer, he recollected, seemed a bit thin and when he opened the abdomen to eviscerate, he noted an enlarged and spotted liver. Nevertheless, he removed the liver. "And no, Doctor, I didn't wear gloves. And no, hunters don't wear gloves. And yes, that's right, the Doctor is not a hunter."

After Ben's disclosure, I called the lab and suggested they make arrangements and precautions for isolating Francisella tularensis bacteria. Tularemia is a rare zoonotic infection often associated with rabbits, but also may be transmitted by deer flies or directly from infected tissue such as the liver, which is often resistant to common antibiotics such as Penicillin. All of Ben's prior therapy was stopped and Gentamicin started intravenously. His temperature declined over the next forty-eight hours, and his appetite returned. Slowly the Francisella tularensis bacteria grew in the blood sent to the state microbiology lab. Two weeks later his serology converted positive, confirming infection. Ben was the only reported case in Virginia that year.

Jennifer and the medical student were present for Ben's discharge conference. A large intravenous catheter was placed in Ben's arm to complete his antibiotic therapy as an outpatient. Ben agreed to return to Selma, my private Winchester office, to allow monitoring of his therapy and care for his IV line. Ben offered to take me deer hunting, but we settled on a nice brook trout as a suitable reward for his recovery.

HUNTED

Mason stood quietly in the thick, snow-covered bushes, small puffs of cloudy white breath escaping from his large nose and bearded face. The temperature hovered at 25 degrees, so even a slight movement made a crunching noise in the crystalized snow. He held his deer rifle ready, fully loaded, the safety free. Mason's ten-year-old son, Frank, stood next to him, alert, the rifle large in his boyish arms. Their eyes were not on each other or their rifles, but on the forest clearing beyond, scanning, ready for the careful deer to lope by.

Mason was a true countryman. He hunted for food, mainly deer, but also rabbit, turkey, and pheasant. He fished the surrounding mountain streams for trout and small lakes for bluegill and perch. His modest garden supplied the family with fruits and vegetables. When not hunting or fishing, Mason was a skilled brick mason, always more work than time available. His wife, Janet, a hospital nurse, rarely had reason to shop at the market. There was no television in their home.

The lives of the forest animals and fish, the changing seasons, the condition of the woods, the quality of bricks and mortar, his multiple home improvement projects, the education of his son and daughter, and Janet's excellent venison pot roast recipe were all subjects of lively Mason conversations. Mason did not care to talk while laying bricks, or for that matter, while scanning the woods for deer. He considered multitasking "multifoolish," a good way to spoil a fine thing. He never hunted for sport, but rather for food and necessity.

Mason was a large, imposing man at 6'2", maybe 220 pounds, mostly muscle. His face was framed by a full dark beard, his hair long, but clean and brushed. Frank was a younger version of his father, minus the beard. Frank had serious eyes and a quiet demeanor. Mason and Frank loved the woods and the animals they hunted. While learning to aim and shoot his deer rifle last year, Frank had wounded, but not killed, a deer. Mason insisted they track the animal for two miles even though the temperature was only 15 degrees and the wind biting. Mason instructed Frank that tracking the deer was their responsibility to the animal who would otherwise die a slow and painful death. Their tracking was not random as Mason had a trained eye for animal footprints and traces of blood from the deer's chest wound. He also knew about animal scat and where an injured deer might seek safe shelter for the night.

Mason was at my country rural home to repair damaged brick patio mortar. We shared a cup of hot coffee while discussing the fine points of mortar color and texture.

"Well, that's about it, Doc. I can't work further this week or next as I have a big project up in West Virginia. Very wealthy DC attorney and developer. He's helping me, unfortunately. He doesn't know much about bricks and mortar or building in general, but he's building this 10,000-square-foot log cabin with a giant brick patio. He drives up from DC, we work like mad for a week, then he goes back to the city."

"What's he do, Mason?" I asked.

"Builds shopping centers and office buildings. He owns lots of homes, many cars, and is on his third wife," he replied.

"Do you teach him about building as you go along?" I asked.

"Ha! That's a good one, Doc. You don't really teach this guy anything, as he knows everything already. Big Plato fan. Quotes *The Republic* while we're laying brick. 'Mason,' he'll say, 'all knowledge is within you, you just have to know the right questions.' He calls the questions dialectic. I call it irritating. Just pay attention to what your eyes and hands are telling you," he explained.

"How does he plan to use the mega cabin?" I asked.

"He owns 10,000 acres of virgin forest, too. He uses the land to hunt, or rather really just to kill. This guy travels all over the world to collect the animals he's shot. He goes to Africa twice a year. Often he hires private guides in private reserves, then ships the trophy heads home. That's how he plans to outfit each cabin room: the lion room, heads of buffalo, antelope, and rhino in other rooms. Even the bathroom will have the head of a monkey watching you pee. Terrible thing. He treats animals as if they existed only so he can hunt and kill them for his personal pleasure. Life is all about him."

"Will you hunt with him?" I asked.

"Oh, that's a big issue. Frank and I know the woods and streams of West Virginia backward and forward. We hunted his 10,000 acres before he bought it. He wants us to guide him on a private hunt, looking for an eight-point buck," he replied.

"Are you going to do it?" I asked.

"His woods are full of deer, wild turkey, rabbit, and all sorts of wild life. No one else hunts this area. So it's tempting. But I don't trust the guy. He doesn't respect nature—he uses it. We'll see."

Weeks passed, Mason more consumed with the mega cabin than he'd planned. He returned finally at 8 a.m. Saturday morning to start our patio project. After a couple hours of silent work, we took a coffee break.

"How's the mega cabin going, Mason?" I asked.

"Good, good. Coming along," he responded.

"Did you go hunting with your boss?"

Mason was quiet for a while, took a deep sigh, then started his account.

"Yeah, we took him up on his offer. Frank and I met him at his cabin at 7 a.m. last Saturday. He was outfitted like a big-game hunter, L. L. Bean boots and all. He's a short guy, but solid. Works out at a gym all the time. Bald as a bowling ball. Shaves his head, too. He had a rifle that could kill a charging elephant. I asked him why he needed such a big gun. He said he only wanted to take one sure shot at the buck. He just needed the buck's head. I could have what's left of the body."

"How'd it go?"

"Frank and I got our limit, a doe each, great for our fine winter feast. We took the deer back to the house and prepared them for the freezer. Didn't see another hunter or soul all day."

"And the Boss?"

"Ah, strange man and got stranger as we went along. He shot at anything and everything—deer, turkey, squirrel, even an owl. Just blew them away. I hated for Frank to see the carnage. He never stopped to check the animals, just kept marching through the woods, looking for his buck and talking about Plato. "Mason," he said, "there are people to work and be governed, and then there are a few select to govern. The thinkers. I'm one of the chosen to rule. We own and guide the rest. Socrates introduced the idea of the philosopher king and Plato made it known through his books to the world. We've lost this most profound concept of human nature. Instead, we preach ridiculous equality, as if anyone can really believe that. Look around you! Are we equal? The guys that do my plumbing, roofing, carpentry, electrical work, even my accountants and lawyers are just tradesmen; they know just one thing— what their senses tell them is true. No big picture, no overview of the world, no insight into the true nature of being and society. Get up in the morning, eat their breakfast, kiss their equally slow wife, labor all day, drink all night. These are the heroes of democracy, the prophets of our future. I don't think so, Mason. These prophets are closer to the woods animals than to epiphany.'"

"I bet he likes Ayn Rand as well?" I asked.

"Oh, right on, Doc. Right after Plato! Survival of the fittest. And he is Uberman. Life revolves around him."

"Did he get his eight-point buck?"

"Yeah, he got him. Ruined the animal, but the head and ant-lers were intact. We loaded everything in the trailer behind my SUV."

"Then?"

"Oh, man, Doc, this is the strangest story. You got to keep this to yourself. I'm a bricks-and-mortar guy right? Not superstitious or religious, really. But here it goes. I'll tell you the first part, what I saw and heard with my own eyes and ears. But the last part, the strange part, I'll relate what the Boss told me after the accident."

"The accident?"

"We're driving home in the dark—guns, gear, and animals loaded up. We're on a curving, narrow, back road. I'm at the wheel. Hard to see with the snow, ice, fog, and shadows. They're out of the woods in an instant: six deer sprinting across the frozen road. I turn quickly to the right and slam on the brakes. We miss them all but the last doe. You know how beautiful and agile they are in the wild—loping, gliding, graceful—thin legs hitting the ground all at once, then bounding up almost as soon as they touch ground. All brown except for a little patch of white on her tail. The front bumper hits her on the left side flank, knocking her up in the air. Then thud! Down on the pavement. We pulled to a halt. Frank's in the back seat, strapped in, like I told him. But the Boss, sitting beside me, undid his seatbelt to get a better angle on cleaning his gun. The quick stop threw Boss and his gun forward. I guess the gun caught him square in the forehead. He's out for about thirty seconds. Then he comes back, groggy. Frank and I jump out of the car to check the deer, but she hobbles up to her feet and limps off the road to follow her family. I turn to the Boss who's just come out of the car, holding onto the door, and Frank, and tell them we have to track the deer—she's badly injured. Frank goes to the trailer to get our guns, but the Boss leans over and throws up. Says he has a terrible headache and he'll stay in the truck and try to sleep it off.

"So Frank and I get our flashlights and guns to track the injured deer in the snow and dark. It's not hard really; she's bleeding pretty bad. We hike across a large field. The other deer are waiting for her on the far side of the field, but when they see us and our lights they scatter. There's a small grove of trees on the far edge of the field with a soft bed of long grass underneath, shielded from the wind and snow by the tree overhang. She's lying in the grass, panting with pain. I aim my rifle at her heart. But it's strange, Doc, real strange—she turns her head and looks me right in the eye. Never had a deer actually focus on me. Almost as if she knew me and knew what I had to do. After I shot her, we carried her back to the truck, and then I opened the cab door to see how the Boss was doing."

"Was he OK?"

"He was drenched in sweat. I don't mean just dripping from his face. I mean he had sweated through his shirt and his hunting jacket. His face was flushed, and he was panting like a runner. And he was holding his left side with his right hand. His forehead had a huge, blue bump where the rifle struck him. I gently shook his shoulder, and he awoke with a scream."

"What did he say?"

"From here, Doc, I'm going to let this be in his words, as best I remember them. 'Oh God, Mason! Oh my God! I'm so glad to see you! Are you and Frank okay?'

'Yeah, we're okay, Boss. How about you? That's a nasty bump on your head.'

'Yeah, my head hurts, but my side is killing me. You won't believe what happened after you left. I climbed back into the truck, laid my head back, then fell into a deep sleep. Then I awoke suddenly. It was quiet, and I could tell I was back in the woods. I was very cold. The snow crunched if I moved just a little. I could see my breath and through the fog the deer waiting on the other side of the field. I started to walk, but my side hurt too much. I quickly became exhausted. I saw a flash of light close by. The deer scattered, frightened. I just had to lie down. I found a small grove of trees and laid in the soft grass underneath. Then I heard you and Frank approaching, tracking the injured deer. I could see your flashlights as you crossed the field, coming closer.'

'My side was killing me. I tried to reach over to my wound, but my arms and legs wouldn't move. I bent my neck down to see the flank wound, and there was blood everywhere. My blood. Then I noticed the hair around the flank wound, fine, tightly woven, smooth hair—not like my hair. I tried again to move my legs and noticed the hoofs, the pointed, cloven foot. Then I heard your boots on the crunching snow. My mouth was parched. I was terrified. I struggled to move, to speak, to yell out to you. The flashlight struck my eyes, partially blinding me, but still I saw your rifle come to your shoulder. I tried to scream, "Mason, it's me! Don't shoot!" I turned my head to look at you just as you pulled the trigger, and I felt the hot pain of the bullet piercing through my chest muscle, then into my heart. Everything went black, silent and numb, except for this terrible pain in my left side. Then I felt your hand on my shoulder, and I began to wake up.'"

"I hope you took him straight to the ER, Mason," I said. "He'd had a bad head injury, probably a concussion."

"We turned around and headed straight to the Winchester ER. No one spoke. Boss seemed to pass out again, holding his side, groaning in his slumber. When we got to the ER we got out of the truck, and I helped Boss walk slowly to the front door. The nurses were rushing toward us with a wheelchair. Just as the ER doors opened, the light hit us full in the face, and Boss turned to me and said, "Oh my God, Mason, what have I done?"

AN ANGEL

Helen sat alert in the large, old red chair in my medical office. She was in her mid-fifties, fit but not athletic, hair short and dark, but styled, British in speech and dress, quick to smile, direct, intelligent, with piercing blue eyes. Her own medical problems dispensed with, Helen now wished to discuss her husband's condition. At an earlier appointment, Ken had given his permission to be open with his wife of thirty years. Ken had advanced congestive heart failure which limited his previously vigorous lifestyle. A former captain in the Navy, Ken had been both a capable sailor and commander as well as a tough combatant. He strained under the limitations of his illness.

"So we're done with me, are we?" asked Helen.

"Yes, you're doing fine, Helen. Your blood pressure is now under control. I think leaving the night wards is helping." Helen was a surgical nurse, as tough and resourceful as her Navy husband.

"I have a favor to ask of you, Doctor A.," requested Helen, eyes twinkling.

"OK," I replied.

"You know how Ken loves to sail, something he hasn't been able to do for several years because of the CHF. Now he is afraid to even try again. And he wants desperately to take our grown son Rob sailing in Bermuda. Ken and Rob have been estranged for years, and Ken thinks this trip might be his last chance to right a wrong, erase a life barrier," she said.

"Why is there a barrier, Helen?"

"It goes way back to when Rob was a teenager. He'd just gotten his driver's license. We had a strict rule that the first six months of driving you had to drive alone. No distracting friends along. Worked fine with his sisters. But Rob is just like his father, headstrong and willful, rebelling against any restraint of his freedom. So of course he eventually asked his three best friends to hide in the bushes one morning so he could give them a lift to high school. Just so happened, our retired neighbor, who rose at dawn to drink her coffee and survey the neighborhood, observed the entire heist, pickup and all, and immediately called me."

"And then?"

"And then I told Ken when he returned from work. He worked himself into a regular huff. Ken was a by-the-book naval captain, after all. Ken lectured Rob about honesty and responsibility; Rob finally had had enough and shot back at his father, 'If these qualities are so important to you, why do you still finish off a full pack of cigarettes each and every day knowing honestly, Dad, they're going to kill you some day.'"

"Well, Ken didn't tolerate backtalk from anyone and struck out with a quick right hand to Rob's face."

"Rob was a big boy, strong as a bull. I think he thought for a moment about hitting back, but then stared his father straight in the eyes and said, "Do that again Dad and it will come right back at you."

"You think Ken made too much of a minor teenage act of independence?" I asked.

Helen laughed.

"Well, yes, don't you? So now, twenty-two years later, they rarely talk, only good in a room together occupied by others, usually my daughters and me. Oh, Ken wants so much to cross the barrier, take Rob on a boat, pass a little good time together, apologize in his own very slow way. But his heart scares him. He had one bad episode of shortness of breath at night. I thought we might really lose him then. That was the night we met you in the ER. You stayed with us until the meds kicked in, the fluid left him, and he finally fell asleep. He's trusted you ever since then. I want you to get him ready, physically and emotionally, to take the sailing trip. Will you do this for us?"

I paused. Much was at stake. I knew Ken would never go back to the hospital. He could die with the strain of sailing again. And yet, there was a chance to redeem a mistake and perhaps to die later at peace with his son and his wife.

"That's a big order, Helen, but yes, I'll try. You know he might not make it; his heart failure is real."

"Yes, oh yes, but I just know you, Dr. A. You're good. You'll do it." Helen clasped her hands together then kissed me on the cheek.

"Helen, you are an angel," I said.

Ken came to our medical office weekly for six weeks. I adjusted his medications, encouraged his ambition, and started a gentle, observed exercise program and gave him intravenous furosemide, a powerful diuretic, to help him lose some excess weight. As his weight fell, Ken's shortness of breath lessened. The exercise program gave him back confidence and optimism. He studied his old sailing books; he was quietly ecstatic that his son had accepted the invitation to spend a long weekend ocean sailing with his father. We both understood the risk that he might die on the sailboat. The last week of Ken's treatment I extracted a promise that he would contact a physician in Bermuda if his chest pain reoccured. Ken smiled after agreeing and said, "I have to do this. I am going to do this!"

Ken and Rob's sailing trip went better than expected. The wind blew, but not too much. The father's knowledge complemented the son's strength. As the trip ended, Ken was able to acknowledge and apologize for his temper. As they parted at the airport, Rob embraced his father and said, "I love you, Dad."

Several weeks after the trip, Helen sat primly in my office, all smiles.

"You did well, Dr. A. The trip was a big success. Ken is so happy, he even took me out to dinner and a movie. So I'll help you with a problem I know you're struggling with:your faith. You just can't see how life and death all fit together."

"How do you know these things, Helen? Yes, I'm struggling with my faith. Are you really an angel?" I asked.

Helen sighed, gazed out the window of my office, framed by a stained-glass window designed to reflect the beauty of the spiral helix of DNA.

"We're not supposed to talk of our gifts, you know. Part of the angel's code," Helen replied.

"What are you saying, Helen? Is your gift to see into our souls, our doubts, our longings?"

"Yes, that is the gift—came upon me early one morning, like an electric shock. One moment I was an irascible, sarcastic woman, and the next a hand of God. Of course, what we do with the insight is up to us. God provides the pathway, but you still have to walk the road. And the gift only works when you're helping others. No stock forecasts, gambling wins, or playing the ponies, which I used to love." Helen laughed her soft chuckle.

"Now back to you, Doctor. You are good at turning conversations away from yourself. This week, one night you will fall into a deep sleep and a dream, really a vision, will come to you. I hope the vision will give you some clarity and peace. But we will never speak of this again, nor to anyone else until after I die. I'm going out on a limb for you," she explained.

AN ANGEL

The week was our usual doctor race of twelve-hour days, night call, interrupted sleep, patient concerns, details upon details. Then on Friday night, the call beeper turned off, a generous wifely back rub, a warm, quiet room, and at last a deep sleep. Then a dream like no other came upon me.

I was walking at night along a narrow trail that meandered through a deep woods. After walking quietly for a few minutes, a young boy emerged from the woods and motioned me to follow him. The boy was lean, agile, and dark skinned, with a radiant smile. He led us through multiple turns and trail forks and eventually to a large clearing in the woods. He motioned to a shadowed crescent at the edge of the clearing and indicated with a motion of his hand for me to lie down in the shadow crescent facing the open clearing. When I was lying down, the boy silently faded back into the woods. The clearing was illuminated by a full, bright moon and a bright star slightly below the moon. The night was warm and still, and I felt my entire body at perfect ease.

The boy reappeared at the edge of the woods, leading a middle-aged man with white and black hair, a stooped posture, and shuffling gait. The boy gently helped the man lie down in the light in the middle of the clearing. Slowly the man's body decomposed into dust, eventually merging with the soil. Over time the boy lead five additional people to the clearing to lie quietly in the light, then dissolve to dust.

Then the boy brought down the path someone very different. The man seemed like a rabid dog, constantly in motion, snapping at the air with an open, salivating mouth. His face was contorted in an angry grimace and his arms twitched in agitation. As though reluctant to cease his pacing, the rabid man eventually laid down in the clearing and shook his arms at the star. Almost imperceptibly, a faint glow of the outline of a spirit emanated from the twitching body. The spirit was as restless as the prone body. The spirit briefly took on a definite form, the man's face transforming from an expression of anger to one of amazement, then profound fear. Gradually the spirit faded into the darkness and the star, which had become faint, resumed its glow.

The night was peaceful for a long time. Then the boy reappeared, leading a slight, fair woman by the hand. Her face was kind but deeply lined with care and age. The boy was especially gentle and careful as he helped the woman lie upon the ground so recently possessed by other souls. Similar to her predecessors, a faint spirit rose from her prone body. The spirit pivoted to the star which began to glow. The spirit's arms extended out as if to hug the night, then gradually faded as the star grew brighter. The boy appeared at the edge of the shadow and motioned for me to follow him. Back through the woods we followed the twisting path until at last in a morning fog we appeared at the wood's edge. The boy waved me on, with just a slight movement of his hand and a faint smile upon his lips. I slept deeply the rest of the night, requiring two pushes of the snooze alarm to at last fully reenter the conscious world.

Ken and Helen did well together for several more years. Then one night Ken had crushing chest pain and shortness of breath and died before the rescue squad arrived. Helen was at his bedside.

Helen moved back to Washington, DC to be with her son and daughters. Several years later, she died rapidly of metastatic breast cancer, surrounded by her devoted family. In her obituary in *The Washington Post*, her daughter celebrated Helen's kindness and uncanny ability to sense the needs of others and lend a helping hand. "Almost like an angel," her daughter reflected.

BIOGRAPHY

Dr. Jack Armstrong studied medicine at the University of Michigan Medical School in Ann Arbor, Michigan. He was trained in epidemiology at the Centers For Disease Control in Atlanta, Georgia, and received additional training in tropical medicine at the LBJ Tropical Hospital in Pago Pago, Samoa. He completed both an internal medicine residency and an infectious disease research fellowship at the University of Michigan. He was honored as a Fellow in the American College of Physicians and the Infectious Disease Society of North America. In 2014, he received the prestigious Laureate Award for lifetime service from the American College of Physicians. He was the Chairman of the Infection Control Committee at Winchester Medical Center from 1978 to 2015.

His private internal medicine and infectious disease practice was located at Selma Medical Associates in Winchester, Virginia. He is a past member of the Virginia Board of Medicine and past president of both Selma Medical Associates and the Infectious Disease Society of Virginia. Although Dr. Armstrong has numerous prior scientific publications, *Lion in the Night* is his first work of fiction.